"You could marry me...."

Freddy said it dizzily, opening eyes with dilated pupils, and registering that she was lying on her back looking up at Jaspar without any recollection of having moved.

Stunning golden eyes, enhanced by spiky ebony lashes, widened as they gazed down on hers with transfixed attention.

"Secretly," Freddy added. "Hide me. I'd keep quiet and look after Ben and then, when the time's right, you divorce me."

Jaspar watched her big aquamarine eyes drift closed and a vague sphinxlike smile curve her lush mouth. Marry her in secret and hide her? She could not demand such an act of insanity and personal sacrifice from him....

Dear Reader,

Last year I read a touching newspaper story about two sisters who had been separated as children and then reunited as adults. That article sparked off the idea for this trilogy. Broken relationships and adoption can lead to siblings losing touch with each other through no choice of their own.

Each book deals with the different life experience of three sisters and the men they love—Freddy, who has initially no idea that she has sisters, Misty, who grows up in care and Ione, who was adopted.

As you'll find out through reading this series, their mother actually made a second marriage. Could it be that there are more stories to come?

Lynne Graham

Lynne Graham

AN ARABIAN MARRIAGE

SISTER BRIDES

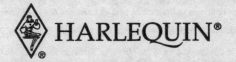

HARLEQUIN®

TORONTO • NEW YORK • LONDON
AMSTERDAM • PARIS • SYDNEY • HAMBURG
STOCKHOLM • ATHENS • TOKYO • MILAN • MADRID
PRAGUE • WARSAW • BUDAPEST • AUCKLAND

ISBN 0-373-12271-3

AN ARABIAN MARRIAGE

First North American Publication 2002.

Copyright © 2002 by Lynne Graham.

Visit us at www.eHarlequin.com

Printed in U.S.A.

CHAPTER ONE

'It is a matter of family honour...' King Zafir's voice was thin and weak but fierce longing burned in his gaze as he addressed his only surviving son. 'You will bring your brother Adil's son home to us and we will raise him to adulthood.'

Crown Prince Jaspar murmured tautly, 'Father, with all due respect, the child has a mother—'

'A harlot *unfit* to be called a mother!' In a sudden explosion of anger, King Zafir raised himself from the pillows and thundered, 'A shameless creature who danced until dawn while her child fought for his life in hospital! A greedy, grasping Jezebel...' At that point a choking bout of serious coughing overcame the irate older man and he struggled in vain to catch his breath.

Instantly, the King's medical team was rushed in to administer oxygen. Pale and taut, dark eyes intent, already stunned by the furious outburst that had brought on the attack, Jaspar watched the physicians go about their work and willed his parent to recover. '*Please*, Your Royal Highness,' his father's closest aide, Rashad, begged with tears in his strained eyes. 'Please agree without further discussion.'

'I had not realised that my father held Western women in such violent aversion.'

'His Majesty does not. Have you not read the report on this woman?'

As he registered in relief that his father was responding to the treatment the worst of the tension holding Jaspar's lean powerful frame taut ebbed and he breathed in deep. 'I have not.'

'I will bring the report to your office. Your Royal Highness.' Rashad hurried off.

A thin hand beckoned from the great canopied bed. Jaspar strode forward and bent down to hear King Zafir's last definitive words on the subject, uttered in a thready tone of deep piety that nonetheless held a rare note of pleading. 'It is your Christian duty to rescue my grandson...'

As soon as the immediate emergency was over and his father had been made comfortable, Jaspar left the room. As he crossed the anteroom beyond, every person there dropped down on their knees and bent their heads. In receipt of that respectful acknowledgement of his recent rise in royal status, he clenched his strong jawline even harder. Reflecting on the recent death of his elder brother, Adil, who had been Crown Prince since birth, only made Jaspar feel worse than ever.

One day he would be King of Quamar but he had not been brought up to be King. In the instant that Adil had died, Jaspar's life had changed for ever. He had loved his brother but had never been very close to him. Adil had, after all, been fifteen years older and cut from a different cloth. Indeed, Adil had often cheerfully called his younger brother a killjoy. But, almost inevitably, Adil's excessive appetite for food and fat Cuban cigars had contributed to his early demise at the age of forty-five.

In the splendid office that was now his, Jaspar studied an oil painting of his jovial brother with brooding regret. Adil had also been an unrepentant womaniser.

'I adore women. *All* of them...' Adil had once told Jaspar with his great beaming smile. 'My wife, my ex-wives, my daughters included, but why should I settle for only one woman? If only we were Muslim, brother, I might have had four wives at a time and a harem of concubines. Do you never think of what life might have been like had our honoured ancestor, Kareem I, not founded us as a Christian dynasty?'

So, when Adil had not been carrying out his duties as Crown Prince, he had sailed his pleasure yacht, *Beauteous Dreamer*, round the Mediterranean with a string of beautiful fun-loving Western women aboard. Rumours of his eldest son's discreet double life had occasionally caused King Zafir great disquiet but Adil had always been a most gifted dissembler and his women had always been willing to cover his tracks for him.

It seemed painfully ironic that the much-wanted son which Adil had failed to father with any of his three successive wives should have been born out of wedlock. Had that child been born within marriage, he would have been second in line to the throne but his illegitimacy barred him from what should have been his rightful place in life. Jaspar suppressed a heavy sigh. In his generation, the al-Husayn royal family had had little luck when it came to producing male heirs, although, having fathered several daughters, Adil had remained excusably optimistic that a son would eventually be born.

And just two years ago, a baby boy *had* been born to an English woman in London. During the hours that Adil had survived before the second heart attack had struck and proved fatal, he had confessed that shocking fact to their distraught father. Unsurprisingly, the news of that unknown grandson had become an obsession with the grieving older man but extensive confidential enquiries had been required even to track the woman down. In fear of a scandal that would reverberate all the way back to Quamar, Adil had gone to considerable lengths not only to disassociate himself from that birth, but also to conceal all evidence of the child's existence.

It was a mess, an unholy mess, that he was being asked to sort out, Jaspar reflected bleakly as Rashad scurried in with much keen bowing and scraping to deliver a sealed file to his desk. His parent was too ill to be made to consider practicalities, but to bring Adil's child back to Quamar, shorn of the supposedly unsuitable mother, would be very difficult, if not impossible.

'His Majesty has made a most clever suggestion which would solve all the problems at once, Your Royal Highness,' Rashad announced in a tone of excitement.

Jaspar regarded the older man in polite enquiry but with no great hope for Rashad was his father's yes-man, guaranteed to always agree with and support his royal employer's every spoken word.

'We use our special forces and *snatch* the child...'

Jaspar drew in a very deep and necessary breath of restraint. Sometimes, his father astounded him. A feudal ruler from a young age, his exalted parent had never quite come to terms with the reality that a very different world lurked beyond Quamar's borders.

'There would be no need to negotiate with the foreign Jezebel and the boy would be whisked back to Quamar, renamed and raised as an orphan. Perhaps we could say that he is a distant cousin's child,' Rashad completed with immense enthusiasm.

Only the fond memory of Rashad playing with him when he was a child himself prevented Jaspar from venting his incredulous dismissal of such an outrageous suggestion. Rashad was not a clever man and he was out of his depth, his sole motivation being a desperate desire to tell his ailing royal employer what he most wanted to hear. As for his honoured parent and sovereign, Jaspar reflected in rueful exasperation, illness and grief had evidently temporarily deprived the head of the house of al-Husayn of his usual common sense and caution.

'Please inform His Majesty that the situation will be resolved without the need for such a dramatic intervention,' Jaspar stated drily.

'His Majesty fears that he will die before he ever lays eyes on the child,' Rashad lamented emotively.

Jaspar was well aware of that fact but also convinced that his father would soon recover his once excellent health if only he would stop fretting himself into pointless rages and thinking of dying. Casting open the file, he expected to see a photo of a leggy brunette of the type his late brother had appeared to find irresistible but there was no photo of either mother or child. So eager had the private detective been to report back on his success in locating the woman that he had wasted no time in gathering supporting evidence.

The child's mother, Erica Sutton, had been christened Frederica, and her own mother had deserted her and her father within weeks of the birth of her twin sisters. At eighteen, Erica had left home with a neighbour's husband in tow but that liaison had soon ended. Becoming a model but rarely working, she had then gone on to enjoy numerous affairs with wealthy married men.

When Erica had given birth to a child, nobody had had the slightest idea who had fathered him, but his mother's newfound financial security had been marked by her purchase of a palatial apartment and the high-spending lifestyle of a party girl in constant search of amusement. As Jaspar read on, his lean, darkly handsome features grew steadily more grave. He was appalled by what he was learning and was no longer surprised by his father's rage and concern. Taking the easy way out of an embarrassing predicament, Adil had left his infant son to the care of a cruelly irresponsible and selfish young woman, who appeared to have not the smallest maternal instinct.

Thrusting aside the file in disgust, Jaspar had not the

slightest doubt that it was his duty to remove his nephew from such an unsuitable home. That a devoted nanny had evidently protected the child from the worst of his mother's excesses was of little consolation, for a nanny was only an employee whose services might be dispensed with at any time. The little boy was at undeniable risk both emotionally and physically in his current environment, Jaspar conceded grimly.

His father had spoken wisely and Jaspar was ashamed that he had set such little store by the older man's outraged condemnation of the child's mother. The only solution *was* for his nephew to be brought out to Quamar. However, and Jaspar allowed himself a wry smile, he would achieve that feat without resorting to springing melodramatic manoeuvres with the army's special forces and causing a diplomatic furore.

Frederica Sutton, known as Freddy since the age of eight and by her own choice, passed the letter from Switzerland over to the grey-haired older woman seated across the table from her. 'What am I going to do now?'

Donning her spectacles and looking very much the retired schoolteacher that she indeed was, Ruth scanned the few lines with a frown. 'Well, that's that, then. You've exhausted every avenue—'

'The *only* avenue.' Freddy's sole lead had been the Swiss bank account from which her late cousin, Erica, had received her generous income.

She had written to the financial institution concerned, explaining the circumstances in some detail. She had hoped that she might somehow establish even third-party contact with whoever had originally set up that payment system. Unfortunately, the cagey response she had received had made it painfully clear that the tenet of client confidentiality forbade any such sharing of information while adding that any more approaches from her or indeed anyone else would be a complete waste of time.

'It's hardly your fault that Ben's father didn't make provision for the reality that at some stage there might be a genuine need for further contact,' Ruth Coulter mused ruefully. 'Possibly he was making it clear that he wanted no more involvement under any circumstances...and who could have dreamt that a woman as young as Erica would die?'

At that reminder, Freddy's aquamarine eyes clouded and she bent her blonde head until she had got her emotions back under control. Her cousin, Erica, had been only twenty-seven when she had met her death on the ski slopes in an accident that could have been avoided. But then Erica had died much as she had lived, Freddy conceded reluctantly, as though every day might be her last, running risk without thought and never, ever thinking of the future.

'I know you miss Erica.' The older woman gave Freddy's hand a brief bracing squeeze. 'But it's been six weeks now and life has to go on, most particularly where Ben is concerned. I doubt if you will ever learn *who* his father is but in the long run that may even be for the best. Your cousin wasn't very choosy about her male friends.'

'She was trying to sort herself out,' Freddy protested.

'Was she?' Ruth raised an unimpressed brow. 'Of course, it's wisest not to dwell on someone's failings once they've gone. Naturally one prefers to remember the good things but one might be challenged in this particular case—'

'Ruth...please!' Freddy was sincerely pained by that frank opinion. 'Surely you remember what a dreadful childhood Erica had?'

'I'm afraid I don't have much faith in the fashionable excuses for downright immoral behaviour. Erica brought that poor child into this world only because it *paid* her to do so.' Ruth grimaced, her distaste palpable. 'She lived like a lottery winner on the child support she received from Ben's father but took not the slightest interest in her own son—'

'She put Ben to bed and read him a story for the first time shortly before she died. They *were* beginning to bond—'

'No doubt you shamed and coaxed her into the effort. If Ben's father had not been an extremely rich and evidently very *scared* married man willing to pay heavily for her discretion, Erica would have had that pregnancy terminated,' Ruth opined without hesitation. 'She had no interest in children.'

Giving up on her attempt to soften Ruth's attitude towards Ben's late mother, Freddy got up and knelt down by the little boy playing on the rug. Ben had his little cars lined up. He was dive-bombing them with a toy aeroplane and all the accompanying noisy sound effects. Aware that her hostess was finding the racket something of an irritation, Freddy directed Ben's interest to a puzzle instead and sat by his side until his attention was fully engaged. He was a very lovable child and she adored him as though he were her own. An affectionate and good-natured little boy with dark curls and enormous brown eyes, Ben had been a premature baby.

Freddy had actually been living with Erica by the time that her cousin had gone into labour. Ben had spent the first few weeks of his life confined to an incubator and Freddy had always blamed that unfortunate fact for her cousin's distressing inability to bond with her baby. Over the months that had followed in her role as nanny to Ben, Freddy had tried everything to encourage that maternal bond to develop and had even taken advice from a psychologist on her cousin's behalf. But nothing had worked. Erica had continued to demonstrate little more interest in Ben than she might have done in a strange child passing her by in the street.

'As you can't contact the father, you need to contact the authorities and notify them about the situation,' Ruth advised. 'It's unfortunate that Erica didn't simplify matters by leaving a will but, naturally, once her solicitor has sorted out her estate, everything will go to Ben as well as that continuing income.'

'Ben's going to be a very rich little boy,' Freddy muttered heavily. 'I expect people will queue up to adopt him and social services are bound to look for a family that are already wealthy in their own right. What hope have I got against that kind of competition? I'm single, currently unemployed *and* I'm only twenty-four—'

'You're also that child's only known relative and you've been with him since birth.' But Ruth Coulter spoke as if neither fact that might support the adoption application that the younger woman was determined to make was a source of satisfaction to her. 'I wish you'd never got involved, Freddy. I can't approve of an unmarried woman of your age taking on such a burden—'

'Ben's *not* a burden.' Freddy's chin took on a stubborn tilt.

'You've had no life of your own since you got tangled up with Erica's problems.' The older woman's disapproval was unconcealed. 'She used you quite shamelessly to take care of *her* responsibilities—'

'I was paid an excellent salary to look after Ben,' Freddy reminded her defensively.

'For weeks on end without a break? Day and night and weekends too?' Ruth enquired drily. 'Your cousin took advantage of your good nature and it's no wonder you're now thinking of that little boy as though he was your son. For the past two years, he might as well have been!'

Studying Freddy's now flushed and guilty face, Ruth

compressed her lips. She had once lived next door to the Sutton family and she had known both Erica and Freddy as children. Children who had been forever joking about the foolish fact that they both had the exact same name—Frederica. Their fathers had been brothers and both had named their daughters in honour of a spinster great-aunt in the forlorn hope that they would eventually be enriched by that piece of flattery. As, at that time, the two families had lost touch with each other, the coincidence had not been discovered until years later. When Erica's parents had been killed in a car accident, Freddy's widowed father had taken in his niece and brought her up with his own daughter.

But who could ever have dreamt that that generous act could have ended up working to Freddy's detriment? In Ruth's opinion, even as a child Erica had been dishonest and precocious, essentially shallow in nature but capable of exercising great charm when it suited her to do so. Ruth had not been impressed by Erica's highly coloured stories of her late parents' cruelty towards her, but a lot of people *had* been impressed even though there had been no proof whatsoever to back up her claims. Within the space of six months, Freddy had been the less favoured child in her own home, for Freddy had never been one to push herself forward or flatter.

Having always been very fond of the younger woman, who had lost her own mother at an early age, Ruth had not been as sorry as she felt she should have been when Erica had run off with a neighbour's husband. Ruth had hoped that without her cousin around to hog the limelight, Freddy would grow in confidence. After all, Freddy was a pretty girl but, having had her self-esteem punctured by Erica at a sensitive age, she regarded herself as plain. Ruth was fond of little Ben as well but she was a pragmatic thinker. She did not want to watch Freddy sacrifice her youth and her freedom just to raise Erica's son. Conscious of Ruth's concerned disapproval and discomfited, Freddy left rather earlier than usual and caught the tube back to her late cousin's apartment. For an instant, entering the spacious hall which gave only a tiny taste of the opulence yet to come, Freddy felt spooked. At any minute she expected Erica to drawl from the drawing-room, 'Is that you, Freddy darling? I have the most horrible hangover. My appetite will need tempting tonight...or do you think I ought to settle for a hair of the dog that bit me? Do you think sobering up was the mistake?'

Her eyes stung with tears afresh. She had known Erica's faults, had often despaired over her cousin's self-destructive habits, but had continued to love her like a sister. In the right mood, Erica had been tremendous fun to be around and if she had been around a lot less than Freddy had wished since Ben's birth, who was to blame for that?

The Arab Prince whom Erica had insisted had fathered Ben? No, Freddy hadn't believed that particular story, most especially not when Erica had got *really* carried away and had added that one day her child's father would be a king! So she had never shared that colourful tale with Ruth. It was just possible, however, that Ben's father had been a rich Arab tycoon, the old geezer with the yacht and the taste for floating floozies whom Erica had been equally indiscreet about mentioning. But a royal prince...no way!

'It's time for your bath,' she told Ben, leading him through to the bathroom off the nursery.

'Boats!' Ben exclaimed with satisfaction, rushing to gather up the plastic collection of toys in the string bag hanging from a hook. 'Me play boats.'

'And then we'll have supper.'

'Love you...' Ben wrapped two small arms tight round Freddy's knees and hugged her with all his might.

Her eyes prickled like mad and she was furious with herself. She was going to lose Ben. Waiting in hope of a helpful response coming from that stuffy Swiss bank had been foolish. There was no point kidding herself or trying to avoid the next step of notifying the authorities so that they could make legal decisions on Ben's behalf. But if only it hadn't been for all that wretched money! However, just as swiftly, Freddy told herself off for resenting the existence of the funds that would enable Ben to have the very best of everything as he grew up. Why didn't she just face it? There was no hope of her being allowed to retain custody of Ben.

She was tucking the little boy into his cot when the phone rang and startled her. Once when Erica had been in residence it had rung off the hook at all hours but as word of her cousin's death had slowly spread the phone had grown steadily more silent.

Answering it, she murmured, 'Yes?'

'I wish to speak to Miss Frederica Sutton,' stated a dark masculine voice with an unmistakable foreign accent.

'I'm Miss Sutton, but *which*—?' Miss Sutton are you asking for, she meant to add.

'Please make yourself available at ten tomorrow morning for my visit. I wish to discuss Benedict's future. I warn you that if any other party is present in the apartment prior to my arrival, the visit will not take place.'

'I beg your p-pardon?' Freddy stammered in her astonishment at those instructions, but even as she spoke the caller concluded the call.

Frowning, she began to put together what she had been told. Had she just spoken to Ben's father? Who else would wish to discuss Ben's future with her? But how had he found out that Erica had died? For goodness' sake, he might even be in regular contact with some friend of Erica's! Or possibly her letter to that Swiss bank had discreetly been passed on even though the institution had officially refused to help. Anyway, what did it matter?

By the sound of it, it very likely *was* Ben's father who was coming to speak to her tomorrow. Who else would be so concerned that there should be nobody else present during their meeting? Who else would demand and require such discretion? Although if that arrogant-sounding character who shot out demands without hesitation was a 'scared' married man, she would not have liked to meet a confident one!

Freddy went to bed that evening in a state of growing anxiety as she tried to imagine what plans the man might have for his secret son. She tossed and turned and wondered whether she ought to wear her nanny uniform and parade her excellent credentials in childcare in the hope of making the best possible impression. But in the end she discarded that idea for she wanted to make known her own blood tie with Ben, slender though it was. And with a rich domineering male, there was too much of a risk that her uniform would encourage him to look on her as a mere employee who could have no possible opinion worth hearing.

So she would put on her only suit and *be* suitably humble while listening, rather than attempting to impose any of her own views. She lay frantically trying to plunder her brain for what little Erica had said about the man who had got her pregnant. 'The kindest man I ever met.' Had her cousin been talking about Ben's father or the Argentinian millionaire who had followed him? Or had the Argentinian preceded Ben's conception?

In the darkness, Freddy blushed for her cousin's many affairs. Erica had been very lovely though, and no doubt it had been hard for her to choose one man, especially when they had nearly always seemed to have a wife in the background. Freddy winced, recalling the times when she had tried to preach moral restraint to Erica and Erica would give her a sad look that had just torn at Freddy's heart and say, 'All I want is someone who will really love me.' And then spoil the effect by adding, 'So what if he belongs to some other woman? Do you think she'd think twice in my shoes? It's a hard world out there!'

By nine the following morning, Freddy was ready for her visitor. The apartment shone because she had got up at six to ensure that not a sliver of dust lurked in any corner. Garbed in a navy suit, white blouse and flat court shoes and with her thick curly blonde hair scraped back into an old-fashioned bun, which she felt gave her a much-needed look of greater maturity, Freddy surveyed her reflection with a critical frown. Then, remembering the spectacles she had once worn for eye strain while studying, she went and dug them out and perched them on her nose. Yes, indeed, she thought with satisfaction, she could easily pass for a sensible young woman of thirty, not that she would lie if questioned, but most probably she would not be asked.

'The kindest man I have ever met,' she kept on repeating to herself to ease her nervous tension. If she could just get the opening, she had lots of arguments to make in her own favour. Ben's father would not need to maintain such a hugely expensive apartment for their benefit, nor would her own living expenses with Ben run to a hundredth of Erica's. If he would only agree to her becoming Ben's legal guardian, she would save him an absolute fortune in all sorts of ways! Please, please, please, she prayed, fingers knotted together as she paced up and down.

And then it finally occurred to her to wonder *how* Ben's father had been able to say that he would not show up if there was anyone else in the apartment. A shiver of belated dismay ran down Freddy's taut spine. The only way he could have uttered that warning would have been in the knowledge that he was having the apartment watched in advance of his own arrival and that was a seriously scary thought! Aware that she had disliked the handful of Erica's male friends whom she had actually met, Freddy suddenly felt quite sick with worry. Ben was adorable but his father could well be a creep or a criminal or both!

The bell buzzed. Sucking in a shaky breath, Freddy went to answer the door. As she stood back, three dark-skinned men dressed in suits and built like human tanks strode into the hall. Completely ignoring her, they proceeded to march into every room of the apartment, evidently checking out whether or not she and Ben were on their own. Surging like a frantic mother hen into the lounge where Ben lay asleep on a sofa, Freddy stood over him, muttering, 'Please go away…please don't wake him up…he'll be scared…I'm scared!'

One of the men spoke into a mobile phone and the trio regrouped together out in the hall while still behaving as if she were invisible. Trembling like a leaf, Freddy folded her arms and listened to the lift arrive with a ping on the landing outside the still-open front door: it was *that* quiet. She heard footsteps, a low exchange of masculine voices and then a tall dark male appeared in the lounge doorway.

He did not look like the kindest man she was ever likely to meet, but she kept on staring like an idiot because he was so incredibly good-looking she was knocked for six. She did not know quite what expectations she had had, but certainly she had assumed he would be a much older man. Not a guy who looked as if he wrestled with sharks for fun before breakfast, ran a couple of marathons before lunch, ruled some vast business empire throughout the afternoon and finished off the day by taking some *very* lucky woman to bed and exhausting her. Caught up in dismay by that last far too intimate thought, Freddy reddened to the roots of her hair.

'You are Miss Frederica Sutton?' he demanded, scanning her with brilliant dark deepset eyes that set her heart racing as if she had just heard a fire alarm.

Freddy nodded in slow motion, her entrapped attention

running over his luxuriant blue-black hair, his fabulous bone structure, the delicious hue of bronze to his complexion, his arrogant nose, his *sinfully* beautiful mouth. He was an absolute pin-up, he was totally fantastic, and Erica must have fallen madly in love with him. Just about any woman would, Freddy reflected dizzily, until she recalled that he was a *married* man and strove in shame to rise above all such inappropriate and personal reflections.

'Speak,' he commanded.

It really *was* a command too, Freddy noted, still searching for her lost vocal cords. He spoke like a male who took it for granted that instant obedience to his every wish would follow. 'I'm Frederica Sutton, just like—' my late cousin, the mother of your child, she had been about to say.

'If I wish to enter a conversation with you, I will inform you,' her visitor drawled, running bold and derisive eyes over her taut figure, his highly expressive mouth curling at the corners. 'I am Jaspar al-Husayn, Crown Prince of Quamar, and I stand here in my brother's place as next closest of kin and uncle to your son, Benedict.'

Freddy's hearing and comprehension seized up and slowed to a snail's pace the very instant he mentioned that he was a prince, a Crown Prince moreover. Erica had not been telling entertaining fibs? Ben's father *was* a royal prince? Silenced by sincere shock at that revelation, Freddy stared, eyes wide and shaken behind her spectacle lenses. But had he not also said that he was Ben's uncle and *not* his father?

'Why have you presented yourself to me dressed in that peculiar way? Do you think to impress me with the belief that you are a good mother? Though it must pain me to be so frank, I am well aware of the life that you lead and equally aware that your ugly appearance can only be a pretence calculated to mislead.'

He did not know that Erica was dead, she registered in

dismay. He believed that she was Erica, got up to be ugly, for some strange reason. *Ugly*. Freddy experienced both anger and pain at that label. No, she knew she wasn't pretty, but it was not good news to hear that a plain suit, a dated hairstyle and a pair of spectacles were sufficient to make her worthy of that cruel word: 'ugly'. He looked like a dark angel, talked like an ignorant, unfeeling louse and probably couldn't pass a single mirror without falling in love with his gorgeous reflection! Was it *his* business that she was not Erica? All that nonsense about discretion and here she was being treated like dirt and he wasn't *even* Ben's father!

'Your brother...' Freddy murmured icily while drawing her slender frame taut to reach her full quota of five feet four inches, her back ramrod straight. 'I'm prepared to speak only to your brother, Ben's father.'

'Adil died of a heart attack last month.'

Freddy frowned at him, her mind struggling to compute the reality that Ben truly was an orphan, that not only his mother but also his father was dead. She swallowed hard, seriously troubled by that news. By some awful quirk of fate, Ben had been deprived of the only remaining individual who had had an indisputable right to make caring choices on his behalf.

'It is I who will take charge of Benedict and remove him from your less-than-adequate care.' And having made that utterly devastating announcement, Crown Prince Jaspar strolled over to gaze down with unfathomable dark eyes at the little boy still curled up asleep on the sofa. 'He is very small for an al-Husayn male. We are a tall family,' he remarked critically.

'What do you mean when you say that *you* are planning to take charge of Ben?' Freddy mumbled, her tummy suddenly behaving as though it were a boat in a storm-tossed sea.

Her imagination was already running riot. She didn't like him and she didn't trust him. What did he mean by that comment that Ben was small? Use your brain and think fast, Freddy urged herself. Her shockingly offensive visitor could only be implying that Ben might *not*, after all, have al-Husayn genes. In other words, he was suggesting that Erica might have lied about her son having been fathered by his brother!

And wasn't it perfectly possible that Jaspar al-Husayn might be hoping that Ben would prove not to be a member of his family? Now that Ben's father had passed away, where did Ben come into the scheme of things? Why would this Crown Prince want to take Ben from a woman he believed to be his mother? Yet in contrast, his brother, Adil, had gone to great trouble to keep his illegitimate son a secret and had pledged a great deal of money to the task of ensuring that the child he'd had no intention of acknowledging would have a financially secure future.

'If you value your present lifestyle and income, don't argue with me,' Crown Prince Jaspar murmured, smooth as silk.

And in that moment Freddy decided that it would be far too risky to disabuse him of his assumption that she was Ben's mother. Not yet anyway. How far could she trust a male who had an advance guard of pure-bred thugs? He might well be a most unsavoury character. Certainly he behaved like one with that threat he had just uttered without conscience, announcing that he had the power to set aside the arrangements that his more responsible brother had put in place. What kind of a man spoke like that when a child's needs and security lay in the balance?

And Jaspar al-Husayn needn't bother looking down that classic nose at her as if she were the dust beneath his royal feet. In fact, Freddy, who had a temper that was usually slow to rise, was just about fizzing with rage in her determination to protect Ben. Only if her concerns were put to rest would she dare to concede the dangerous truth that as Ben's uncle *he* had far more rights than *she* could possibly have.

'Can you offer me proof of your identity?' Freddy enquired, unleashing the first volley of what she expected to be a long and bitter defensive battle.

The brilliant dark eyes flashed gold, lush black lashes narrowing over his piercing gaze. 'I have no need to offer such credentials.'

That rich dark drawl carried a note of incredulity that he could not hide. Freddy straightened her shoulders. 'I don't know you from Adam. You could be anybody and I'm not prepared to discuss Ben's future without evidence that you are who you say you are.'

'I am not accustomed to being spoken to in such a discourteous manner,' Crown Prince Jaspar countered in the most lethal tone.

A chill ran down Freddy's rigid spine but she needed time, time to check him out and time to take advice. That it would mean for ever burning her own boats with this arrogant male was unavoidable, for Ben's safety and well-being were of paramount importance.

'Perhaps you could come back tomorrow evening about eight with appropriate references,' Freddy countered unevenly, somewhat intimidated by the aura of sheer blazing disbelief that emanated from him. 'I will then be happy to sit down and discuss in a polite and civilised way what path his future should follow.'

'You have angered me. You will regret it.' Jaspar al-Husayn swore very softly.

Pale as death, Freddy watched him stride from the room and listened to the front door thud shut in his wake. He had given her such a scare that she could hardly breathe. Ben began to wake up, sleepily rubbing his eyes and whim-

pering a little the way he often did at such times. Freddy
gathered him up in her arms and hugged him to her, her
heart racing. An orphaned child born of such important
lineage and likely to inherit a large amount of money was
a very vulnerable child, she reflected fearfully. She needed
to make an appointment with a solicitor and check out her
legal position.

CHAPTER TWO

LATE afternoon of the following day, Jaspar studied the report from his security team on Erica Sutton's activities since his visit to her apartment. That she had evidently rushed straight to a solicitor for advice came as no surprise to him.

Jaspar was satisfied that he had put Erica Sutton under considerable pressure, which had been precisely his intent. While his late brother had been gracing ceremonial occasions and cruising the Med with his party girls, Jaspar had been acquiring the brilliant business acumen with which he oversaw Quamar's considerable investments abroad. Military school and the tough, fast-moving world of finance had honed Jaspar's natural talents to a fine and ruthless edge. He knew how to negotiate. Once he knew his quarry's weaknesses and the time was right, he moved in for the kill.

Subjecting Erica Sutton to the fear that she might lose all that she had gained by her son's birth had been a deliberate ploy. Doubtless, she imagined that to continue enjoying her present lifestyle she had to retain custody of her son but that was not, in fact, the case. When she learned that she could give up his nephew *without* surrendering her financial security, Jaspar believed that she would rush to do so.

But he was intensely amused to read that Erica had apparently spent two hours in a beauty salon that very afternoon. So the *real* Erica Sutton was about to make herself known! His crack about her unlovely appearance had evidently been more than flesh and blood could stand. Had she imagined when he'd set up that first meeting that he was someone who had power over her finances? Why else would she have gone to such ridiculous lengths to present him with that fake image? How could she have thought that he would be impressed by such a disguise? Adil, connoisseur that he had been, would not have looked twice at a woman with a hideous hairstyle, heavy spectacles and frumpy clothes.

But then, possibly, Erica Sutton was not the brightest spark on the block, Jaspar conceded lazily, recalling the reality that she had telephoned the Consulate of Quamar in an apparent effort to confirm his identity. So naive, so clumsy, he reflected, for naturally even the junior diplomat who had dealt with her call had refused to confirm or deny his presence in London on what was essentially a private trip. But then he was surprised that she had not simply recognised him from the many family photographs on his late brother's yacht, *Beauteous Dreamer*.

Hopefully, he could wrap up the whole unfortunate business by the end of the day for he did not wish to strain his father's non-existent patience. He already had nursery staff standing by to take charge of his nephew. Possibly the arrival of a grandson might distract his parent from the rather more personal goal which Adil's death had sadly made a matter of much greater urgency…Jaspar's *own* marriage.

At thirty years old, he was well aware that he was fortunate to still be single. But then his father had feared that Adil's inability to settle with one woman had been the direct result of having been pressed into marriage while he'd still been too immature to have made that commitment. However, Adil's death had changed the whole picture where Jaspar was concerned. That he marry and produce a son to safeguard the succession was now of great importance.

He would let his father choose his bride. Why not? For

the past two years, the royal household had staged regular social events simply to ensure that he met a great number of young women. On a most discreet basis, innumerable bridal candidates had been served up for Jaspar's perusal, the hope being that he would do what everybody wanted him to do and fall in love. But the knowledge that he was being targeted with every weapon in the feminine armoury had made him extremely critical. And the concept of love left Jaspar colder than Siberian ice. Adil had *always* been falling in love, but Jaspar had only loved once and the experience had been traumatic. Love was a weakness that Jaspar had no intention of falling victim to a second time.

The day before, Freddy had visited the first solicitor able to give her an immediate appointment. Having described Ben's situation without naming names, she had requested an honest opinion of her position.

'An uncle is a close relative and, in this particular case, the authorities would also take into account Ben's inheritance as well as his background,' the older man informed her.

Freddy tensed. 'His…background?'

'Naturally with his father having been of Arabic descent there are cultural aspects which would *have* to be respected in his upbringing.'

Not even having foreseen that likelihood, Freddy paled, but she pressed on regardless to finally reach the climax which she had intended all along. 'But if I was to apply to have Ben made a ward of court…er…to protect him?'

'Protect him?' The solicitor frowned in visible surprise. 'On what grounds? Have you cause to believe that Ben would be at some risk with his uncle?'

'Well, not precisely, but…I didn't like the man *at all*,' Freddy proffered feelingly.

'If necessary, social services would intervene to ensure

the child's well-being but, on the basis of what you've told me about the uncle, I don't see why they should. I also don't think you need to take quite so much responsibility onto your own shoulders,' she was told.

Disconcerted by that quiet rebuke, Freddy left his office, dogged by the depressing suspicion that she had been charging at foolish windmills and refusing to accept the inevitable. *Why* had it not occurred to her that Ben's cultural heritage would weigh heavily in the balance of what was judged best for him? Such an obvious point, yet she had not even recognised it and there was no way on earth that she alone could meet that need.

Arriving back at the apartment, she contacted the Consulate of Quamar to try to verify Jaspar al-Husayn's identity. The man she spoke to was not helpful. However, the internet search she then did on Erica's computer proved more fruitful for the royal family of Quamar had an official website. It contained a small respectful piece on the demise of the former Crown Prince, Adil, and a much lengthier bulletin on King Zafir's precarious state of health. However, her own attention was immediately engaged by the picture of the present heir to the throne, Jaspar al-Husayn, looking impossibly handsome and grave and indisputably the same arrogant male who had visited her.

Totally disheartened by that final confirmation, Freddy went to bed that night and made herself face facts. Jaspar al-Husayn evidently knew enough about her late cousin's lifestyle to have deemed her an unfit parent and could she truly blame him for that? Had she been unfairly biased against him? After all, it had been a considerable shock when Ben's uncle had come out of nowhere to demand him and a hard, hurting blow in terms of her *own* fond hopes of keeping Erica's child, Freddy acknowledged with scrupulous honesty. But it would be very wrong of her to allow selfish personal feelings to blind her to what would be best for Ben.

Ultimately, it seemed, Crown Prince Jaspar would gain custody of Ben and there was nothing she could do about that. However, if she continued, *just* in the short term, to let him believe that she was Ben's mother, she could at least learn what his plans for Ben entailed and try to persuade him to make the break between herself and Ben a gentle one. Then she would have to come clean about only being Ben's nanny and no doubt Crown Prince Jaspar would be absolutely furious with her on that score.

Even as she choked back a sob at the prospect of being parted from Ben, Freddy recognised that it was Jaspar al-Husayn's demand for total discretion that worried her the most. How could he take personal charge of an illegitimate child whose very existence would surely cause an enormous scandal in a conservative Arab country? It was not as though he could adopt Ben: as far as Freddy was aware, Muslim countries did not practise adoption.

Recalling how suspicious the Crown Prince had been of her staid appearance on his first visit, Freddy decided that she had better make what effort she could to look the part she now felt forced to play for a little longer. So the following afternoon she went to get her hair done. Afterwards, she was rather stunned by the foaming mane of eye-catching blonde curls she seemed to have developed.

Freddy had always worn her hair tied back. Indeed, she would have had it cut short had her late father not once remarked on how pretty her hair was. Well, long hair was all very well but not practical during working hours, and long thick curly hair was something else again unless one was talented with a blow-dryer, which Freddy was not.

A couple of early and very wounding experiences with boys had confirmed her conviction that she was a born spinster just as Ruth had once confessed herself to be. In recent

years, only amorous drunks or self-pitying types desperate
for a sympathetic audience had demonstrated any interest
in her. Why? Well, as Erica had said, 'You're a little plump
and homely, Freddy.'

Freddy loathed her body and loved to cover it. A mere
glimpse of her too ample bosom and curvaceous behind
when she was undressing was enough to depress her for
the rest of the day. Developing far in advance of her school-
mates had been a severe embarrassment in primary school
and hiding beneath capacious sweaters and T-shirts had become a necessity when she'd compared her own burgeoning shape to Erica's reed-slender delicacy. No matter how
hard she exercised, her full curves remained.

After tucking Ben in, she hovered by his cot, gazing
down into his peaceful and sleepy little face. Her throat
thickened and she felt as if a giant hand were squeezing
her heart and dared not even think of what her life would
be like without him. She went for a quick shower and then
wound herself into a pink towel. In the cloakroom, she
stood at the vanity unit, which had marvellous lighting, and
painstakingly applied eye-shadow and mascara. She rarely
bothered to use cosmetics yet she knew every trick, lessons
learned by watching Erica as both teenager and woman.

The doorbell buzzed just as she was putting on lipstick.
She smiled because she had ordered herself a pizza as a
treat. Once a week, where was the harm? Taste buds watering, she went to answer the door. It didn't matter that
she was only wearing a towel as the take-away employed
a woman to deliver in the area.

But when Freddy opened the door, she got a surprise.
Jaspar al-Husayn strode into the hall without awaiting an
invitation.

'I thought you were my pizza being delivered,' Freddy
mumbled, aghast at his early arrival and then shocked all
over again by the sheer impact of him in the flesh.

She encountered stunning eyes the colour of pure gold and was dazzled. If I had three wishes, it would be him…and him…and him, she thought dizzily, her heartbeat taking off like a jet plane. Electric tension held her fast and breathing was a challenge. The tall wrought-iron lamp cast shaded light that shimmered over the luxuriant black hair swept back from his brow, accentuated the smooth planes of his hard cheekbones, and lingered on the sculpted curve of his firm male lips.

His lean, tightly muscled frame was sheathed in a dark grey business suit that was exquisitely tailored to his powerful physique. A study in shades of vibrant bronze, he was lethally attractive. And meeting those eyes, those extraordinary eyes that she could not look away from, she felt an enervating charge of tension pulse through her, tautening every tiny muscle. Yet her body was filling with a sensation of liquid, languorous warmth, making her outrageously aware of the heaviness of her breasts and the sudden embarrassing prominence of her nipples.

'Pizza…' Jaspar murmured huskily, rooted to the spot by the sight of her.

Where the hell had his attention been on his previous visit? he asked himself with stark incredulity. Her eyes were the aqua colour of the sea, that curious blending of blue and jade and turquoise that changed according to the light. And she had the kind of hair mermaids had in fairy tales, a wild golden mane that fell round her shoulders in glorious, rippling abundance. But no legendary sea creature could have competed with the luscious swell of her creamy breasts above the towel or that glorious hourglass shape. Even as he hardened in hot-blooded male response to that sensual vision, Jaspar was shifting cool mental gears, knowing that he had severely underestimated the opposition and that was a rare error for him. He wanted to rip the towel off, propel her back against the wall and sink deep into her, lose himself in the kind of raw, urgent sex he hadn't fantasised about since he was a teenager. And maybe he would, once he had got what he wanted.

'P-pizza,' Freddy stammered like a belated echo, dazed by the throbbing silence, the almost painful tension and heat inside her, the sheer terrifying emptiness of her own mind.

'Are you planning to take the towel off?' Jaspar enquired silkily. 'Or are you just a tease?'

Slow burning colour flushed her throat in a wave and climbed up into her cheeks as she tore her dilated gaze from his intent scrutiny and glanced down at herself in dismay, absorbing the fact that she truly was still hovering a few feet from him clad only in a towel. With a stifled moan of embarrassment, she blundered into sudden movement in the direction of the cloakroom.

Afterwards, she could never work out how it happened, but as she accidentally brushed against him he caught her to him, one lean brown hand anchoring into her hair, the other splaying to her hip. Her startled aqua eyes flared into mesmeric gold and it was as if fireworks were flaring inside her, setting every inch of her ablaze.

'The stammer was overkill…' he told her huskily, white, even teeth flashing as he slanted a mocking smile down at her, 'but the welcome invitation was *ace*—'

'You've got the wrong idea!' Freddy gasped, all composure crumbling.

'I don't think so…I hate to sound like a jerk, but women have been throwing themselves at me since I was a teenager.'

And before Freddy could even absorb that unashamed assurance that wickedly sensual mouth had descended with devouring heat down onto hers. Intense excitement surged up inside her in a sheet of multicoloured flame. Reaching out blindly, she gripped his arm to stay upright. She felt as if she were falling, falling so fast and furiously that she would burn up before she reached solid earth again. And nothing mattered, nothing mattered but that that connection with him remained. She was in a wonderland of sensual discovery, gasping at the plundering invasion of his tongue inside the tender interior of her mouth, shivering violently, desperately longing for him to pull her close and crush her up against him.

She heard the doorbell buzz with a kind of delayed recognition only as he tensed and then pulled back from her.

'Oh…crumbs…'she framed, blinking rapidly and then shooting into the cloakroom behind him like a scalded cat.

Thrusting home the bolt on the door, Freddy flung herself back against it, shaking like a leaf in a gale. The mirror surrounded with lights opposite confronted her with her own image. Literally cringing with mortification, she studied her swollen mouth, her dilated pupils and the expression of shock and bewilderment still etched there. How are you ever going to go out there again and act as if nothing happened? screamed the first thought to emerge from her reawakening brain.

He thought she had deliberately flaunted herself in the towel too. True brazen hussy stuff. At that realisation, she writhed in even greater embarrassment, but over and above that discomfiture lurked an entire new level of self-knowledge. She honestly *hadn't* known that a man could make her feel like that. There was a sort of shameless fascination still gripping her: that one smouldering kiss could make her forget everything. Who she was, who he was, *everything*. It also seemed especially cruel that she should have made that discovery with Jaspar al-Husayn. In fact, could there be anything more infuriating? All this time she had wondered why most women's magazines raved about sex as though it was a truly exciting pursuit when her own slender experience had taught her otherwise.

And then this guy she hated like poison grabbed her and showed her that the excitement might actually *not* be a giant con practised on the female sex. How dared he have done that to her? What was the point of finding out that a Crown Prince had more than a fighting chance of persuading her out of celibacy? A blasted Crown Prince, she thought afresh, eyes scorching with sudden tears.

He had come to talk about Ben, she reminded herself. Paling, she forced herself to move and unlocked the door sneakily and silently, before pressing down the handle equally quietly and peering out into the hall through a gap barely an inch wide. The coast seemed clear. Had he left? She crept out and then fled down the corridor to her bedroom faster than the speed of light to find some clothes.

Pulling on an oversized T-shirt and a jersey skirt which fell almost to her ankles, she dug her feet into clumpy shoes. The whole time she was dressing, she was rationalising what had happened between them. He had taken her by surprise. She had been temporarily deprived of her wits by the simple fact that he was so gorgeous. But he only had to speak and his mythical attraction vanished, so really she was quite safe from making an even bigger ass of herself. So women were forever throwing themselves at him...oh, the poor love, how did he bear the torment of being so unbearably fanciable? He had the most gigantic ego and she would have done anything to puncture it.

She trudged back down to the main reception rooms, very much hoping he wouldn't be waiting for her. But the guy had no tact, no shame and the kind of self-assurance that would have ensured that the *Titanic* sank the iceberg instead of the other way round. There he was, large as life and twice as bold in the drawing-room, which she had barely entered since Erica's death. But then he had found his natural milieu, hadn't he? He looked more at home there against the elaborate furniture and the curtaining weighed down with excessive swagging, fringing and tassels.

'Your pizza...' Indicating the shallow box parked on the coffee-table, Jaspar al-Husayn sent her a slow, slashing smile that made her heart skip a beat and told her too many things that she didn't want to know.

'Look, I don't fancy you!' Freddy heard herself state with shocking baldness before she could think better of it. 'So you can stop looking so pleased with yourself because what happened out in that hall was just one of those stupid things and there is not the smallest danger that I am going to be tempted to throw myself at you! Not unless I get a brain transplant.'

He said nothing. In the silence that dragged even in the first second, and which was working like a shriek alarm on her nerves by the tenth second, Jaspar gazed back at her with measuring cool.

Freddy could feel her face burning up like a bonfire. While those ten seconds limped past, she went from defensive defiance to shrinking chagrin. What on earth had come over her? Instead of ignoring what had happened, she had dredged it back up again and attacked him like a teenager desperate to save face.

'Let's discuss my nephew,' he finally murmured in his rich, dark drawl. 'Feel free to enjoy your pizza.'

Freddy pictured an imaginary headline: 'Crown Prince battered to death by pizza box'. She hated him, oh, boy, did she hate him. Every time he opened his mouth, he put her down, and only a minute ago he had proved that he didn't even have to speak to achieve that feat. Freddy plonked herself down on an overstuffed sofa. Her tummy gurgled and she stiffened with embarrassment and stared a hole in the pizza box. She had a healthy appetite and she was starving, but she was convinced that if she started eating he would take one scornful look at her and think, No wonder she's that size!

Mind you, he had kissed her, hadn't he? Her downbent head came up a notch. Obviously he hadn't found her that unattractive. There must have been some spark on his side of the fence. Maybe he *liked* women who weren't skin and bone. It was such a seductive thought that Freddy had an instant vision of herself lying in a desert tent being stuffed with sweets by an adoring male, who would *die* if she mentioned going on a diet. What was the matter with her? For goodness' sake, this was probably the most important discussion she would ever hold in her whole life, for Ben *was* her life, and yet her mind was filled with nothing but nonsense!

'I understood that you employed a nanny for my nephew,' Jaspar remarked without warning. 'Where is she?'

Wondering how on earth he could seem to know so much about Erica's life and yet not know that her cousin was no longer alive, Freddy stiffened and then forced herself to look at him. 'She has a family emergency to deal with right now. Look…you said you wanted to take charge of Ben. I'd like to know why.'

Jaspar al-Husayn surveyed her with narrowed golden eyes. 'He is my nephew.'

'But your brother wanted Ben's existence kept a secret. He didn't seem to want anything further to do with him either.' Freddy was choosing her words carefully.

'I will not comment on my late brother's decisions,' Jaspar murmured, his strong jawline clenching. 'It would be inappropriate.'

'But I don't think it's unreasonable of me to ask *why* you have this sudden desire to give Ben a home,' Freddy persisted.

'I have in my possession a recent investigation report into your lifestyle.'

Instinctively resenting that superior tone as much as she disliked the news that a private detective had been snooping into Erica's life without her late cousin's knowledge, Freddy tilted her chin and said with helpless defiance, 'Bully for you!'

Jaspar dealt her a grim appraisal. 'The report made it clear that you are a neglectful mother. You have continually left my nephew to the sole care of an employee, sometimes for periods of six weeks at a time. When you are at home, you throw wild parties for your drunken friends. The police have been called on more than one occasion to settle violent disputes at this address.'

Freddy reddened with sudden shame because it was all true and she turned her head away for a moment, no longer able to meet his challenging gaze. She could still recall lying nervously awake behind a locked door with Ben on the night that Erica had staged her first party since her son's birth. Neighbours had complained to the police about the excessive noise and offensive behaviour of the guests. When, on a subsequent evening, someone had tried to force their way into the bedroom, Freddy had been really scared. After that experience, whenever Erica had decided to throw a party, Freddy had simply taken Ben over to Ruth's and spent the night there with him in peace.

'I...' She swallowed hard, wondering what on earth she could say in her cousin's defence, but on the score of her constant absences and those rowdy parties there was little she *could* say. 'I can see that it looks bad—'

'It looks worse than bad,' Jaspar interposed with cutting contempt. 'It's obvious that you have no taste for being a mother and even less concern for your child's welfare. Adil's son is an al-Husayn. Honour demands that we now acknowledge *our* responsibility towards him.'

'And who does "we" cover?' Freddy prompted, because she knew he was single after looking at that website. In fact there had been some emphasis on the subject of the current heir to the throne of Quamar still being unmarried. Maybe they were subtly advertising him as being up for grabs, hoping that some veiled Middle Eastern princess of unimpeachable virtue and blue-blooded lineage would apply for the privilege of becoming a queen-in-waiting.

'My family,' Jaspar enunciated with pride.

'But you're single and a young child needs a mother figure,' Freddy pointed out with some satisfaction.

His fabulous bone structure tightened. 'I have many relatives within the extended family circle. I hope that some one of them will offer my nephew a caring home.'

'But *not* you,' Freddy noted, angry at the concept of Ben being casually rehomed with the first party willing to take him in.

'As I am unmarried, it would look very suspicious were I suddenly to produce a child out of nowhere and announce that I intended to bring him up. I am not in a position to even consider that possibility.' Jaspar dealt her a look of flaring impatience, his firm mouth compressing. 'Had I had a wife and had she been willing to enter such a pretence, we might have been able to pass him off as an orphaned relative of hers. But, right now, it is not an option.'

So, although he was Ben's uncle, he would not be personally involved in his nephew's future. Freddy was dismayed. Such a proposition was hardly what she had imagined.

'You must understand that our society is not liberal and discretion is a necessity. My nephew's parentage must be concealed for his own sake. Illegitimacy is still a mark of shame in Quamar,' Jaspar al-Husayn continued with gravity. 'Naturally we also wish to avoid creating a scandal which would cause severe embarrassment to Adil's family.'

From beneath her lashes, she noted the brooding tension

of his stance. 'You resent me asking questions…but I love Ben very much and all I want is what is best for him.'

'In the light of what I know about you, I find that claim difficult to credit.' His lean, strong face set hard. 'You have valued your son not for himself but only for his worth in financial terms. I have little taste for this dialogue with you, so let me assure you that your current income will continue at its present level if you give your son into my care.'

'Whatever you think of me, money does not come into this,' Freddy breathed tightly, her tummy giving a sick little somersault at the idea. 'Ben needs to be loved. All children need to be loved and he's an affectionate child. You talk about honour and responsibility but I'm talking about daily love and support—'

'You have no right to question me in this way. Whatever we offer will be immensely superior to the level of care that Ben currently receives,' Jaspar stated with hard finality.

Freddy snatched in a ragged breath. 'But it will take time for Ben to adapt to a new home and new people.'

'I don't have time to waste. My father is at present ill and most eager to meet his grandson. I would like to fly back to Quamar with my nephew tomorrow.'

'Tomorrow?' Freddy was aghast. 'Ben hasn't even met you yet and you know nothing about him. He's not a parcel you can just lift and toss onto a plane!'

'I have highly qualified nursery staff waiting to take charge of him.'

Freddy shook her blonde head slowly and looked at him with shaken aquamarine eyes. 'You really don't know anything at all about young children, do you?'

'He is still only a baby and he will soon adapt to a new life with caring people,' Jaspar delivered.

'He would be traumatised if he was suddenly taken away from me. He needs to be eased into that transition,' Freddy told him with spirit. 'It can't be done overnight—'

'If the break must be made, it should be quick and clean. I cannot accept that his attachment to you or your attachment to him is of any true consequence,' Jaspar countered with perceptible derision. 'After all, you have spent most of his short life sunning yourself on tropical shores and partying without him!'

Freddy was thinking frantically fast and she came up with what seemed like a solution on the spur of the moment. 'I'd be willing to come out to Quamar with him and stay in a guesthouse or something until he was able to manage without me for longer periods—'

Brilliant golden eyes shimmered over her. 'You're talking nonsense. This is the same child who had to get by without you for weeks on end, and I have no hesitation in telling you that you won't be welcome in Quamar at any time now or in the future.'

He was a bone-deep stubborn male, Freddy registered, her anxiety on Ben's behalf steadily mounting. He had not a clue about children but it was quite beneath him to admit it. He did indeed believe that he could remove Ben from everything familiar without causing him distress. For the first time, it occurred to her that she had made a cardinal error in allowing Jaspar al-Husayn to continue believing that she was Erica. He was all too well acquainted with her cousin's poor record as a parent and it was hardly surprising that he was impervious to her arguments. So did she now tell him the truth?

If she confessed that she was only his nephew's nanny, he would be outraged. He did not strike her as a forgiving type of male. He might feel that she had tried to make a fool of him. He would be furious that he had discussed what he clearly regarded as very private family matters with a humble employee. Worst of all, he would immediately realise that she had no power to prevent him from removing Ben from her care. He might walk straight into Ben's bedroom and just lift him out of his cot without any further discussion, she thought fearfully.

'Tomorrow morning, I will send the nanny here to collect my nephew so that she can spend the day with him and get to know him. Will that satisfy you?' Jaspar asked drily.

Freddy saw that she was fighting a losing battle. She remembered the solicitor who had suggested that she was taking too much on her own shoulders in seeking to interfere and she lost colour at that recollection. How much was she truly thinking of Ben? And how much was her judgement being influenced by her own wants and wishes? After all, she did not *want* to give Ben up and wasn't that very selfish of her?

'Will Ben have proper parents in Quamar?' she whispered shakily.

'Of course. There is more than one childless couple in the family.'

Freddy hung her head, shame enclosing her. Had there ever been grounds for her to suspect his motives in seeking to change his late brother's arrangements for Ben? Wouldn't it have been much more simple for the al-Husayn family to leave those discreet arrangements in place? Even the investigation report that he had mentioned suggested that his family's most driving concern had been for Ben's welfare.

'If it suits,' Freddy muttered tautly as she stood up, 'I'd like to speak to you again tomorrow evening.'

In the hall, Jaspar al-Husayn gave her a keen appraisal. Perhaps she felt that she had to go through the concerned maternal motions, he reflected. Perhaps she couldn't help herself; perhaps, as was often the case, she could not see herself as the appalling parent that she in fact was. But he had won and he knew it. She would give up her rights to her son on his next visit. He was surprised to feel a faint pang of compassion as he scanned her strained face and the tense downcurve of her ripe mouth.

As the apartment door closed behind him a painful shuddering sob broke from Freddy. Ben was as good as gone. When she admitted that she was merely his nanny, who knew what Jaspar al-Husayn would do? He would certainly never accept the strength of the bond between her and Ben. 'If the break must be made, it should be quick and clean.' No, had she confessed her true identity, Ben might have been removed from her care even sooner.

CHAPTER THREE

AFTER a sleepless night, Freddy rose early the next morning.

Every last minute she had to spend with Ben now seemed so impossibly precious. She sat watching him eat his favourite breakfast of a boiled egg with toast soldiers for dipping and her throat closed up so much, it physically hurt. She studied his rounded little face below his dark fluffy curls, the twin crescents of his long lashes, the smooth baby skin still flushed from sleep, and she honestly thought that her heart was going to break.

The night before, she had let herself get all worked up about a stupid kiss probably because it had been easier to concentrate on that foolishness than to face and deal with the loss of the child she loved. But Ben wasn't hers and he never would be hers and somehow she had to learn to accept that and step back. The pain she was feeling now was entirely her own fault. During her training, she had been warned not to make the mistake of forgetting that the child in her care had a mother and that she was only a temporary carer who would inevitably move on to another family. But she had not been able to abide by that rule. Ben had looked to her for love and she had given it to him, rationalising that in Erica's absence, Erica's very unwillingness to make that commitment, someone had to compensate Ben and give him what he needed to thrive.

It had been Freddy who had sat by Ben's incubator hour after hour during the first worrying weeks of his life, Freddy who had ultimately named him after their paternal grandfather when Erica had said she couldn't care less what her son was called. Eyes watering as she forced a smile for Ben's benefit and washed his face and hands, she found herself thinking back to her earliest memories of Erica.

When her widowed father had taken her orphaned cousin into their home, Freddy had been a lonely eight year old. Even then, Erica had been an incredibly pretty girl with an elfin face, catlike eyes and silky dark brown hair. She had had enormous charm as well. She had had the power to make Freddy's dour father laugh and had been wonderful at teasing him out of his bad moods. Admiring Erica for her vivacity and confidence, Freddy had been happy to take a back seat. She had had to get much older before she'd appreciated that, beneath all that superficial sparkle, Erica was quite incapable of being happy for more than a couple of hours or of ever feeling truly secure.

Seven years later, there had been a huge scandal when Erica had run away with a neighbour's husband. Freddy's father had raged at the embarrassment of it all for days on end. Only weeks later, the erring husband had slunk back home again and Erica had attempted the same feat, only to have the door slammed in her face by her uncle. Freddy had been heartbroken that awful night. She had seen the shock and disbelief on Erica's face, Erica who had never ever thought of consequences or of how her actions might have impacted on other lives.

But the following year, Erica had come to see them again. Looking very glamorous and impossibly penitent, she had soon won her uncle's forgiveness and had told them stories about her exciting life as a successful model in London. Stories full of whopping fibs, Freddy had later appreciated, for the truth that Erica had depended on her lovers to keep her would scarcely have been acceptable.

At nineteen, Freddy had gone to college to train as a nanny and, for some time afterwards, contact with her cousin had dwindled to the occasional phone call. However, when Freddy's father had died, Erica had come to the funeral, wan and pregnant and indeed looking anything but well. The cousins had had an emotional reunion and Erica had asked Freddy to come and live with her in London and help her get through the remainder of her pregnancy.

Freddy had not had to think twice about that decision. At the time she had just completed her first job as a nanny and, in the wake of her father's death, she had been ready for a change. Erica had been genuinely ill, suffering from continual nausea and the constant threat of a miscarriage. Her cousin had spent the last weeks preceding her son's birth lying flat on her back in a hospital bed, her only visitor, Freddy.

So, to some degree, Freddy had understood Erica's refusal to relate to her tiny child in his incubator. In so many ways, Erica had never really grown up. Like a kid just let loose from school, Erica's only thought after her delivery had been to regain her figure and reward herself for all those months of sick and joyless boredom. In her mind, Ben had already had too big a slice of her life.

'Why do you think I brought you down here to look after me?' Erica had asked when Freddy had tried to remonstrate with her cousin. 'I know you'll do what I ought to do. You can be his substitute mum.'

'But he needs *you* to love him.'

'I think the only person I have ever loved is you,' Erica had quipped.

Freddy was dredged from her painful memories by the buzz of the doorbell. It was barely nine in the morning and the nanny had arrived to collect Ben much earlier than Freddy had hoped she would. The young woman introduced herself in perfect English as Alula. A slim brunette in her twenties, constrained in her manner and reluctant it seemed to even look Freddy in the face, Alula immediately centred her attention on Ben.

Freddy hovered and answered questions about Ben's dietary preferences and routines that were asked with reassuring professionalism. She scolded herself for feeling uneasy at the brunette's total lack of friendliness. 'Where are you taking Ben?' she asked, trying to sound casual.

'I haven't yet received instructions.' Alula knelt down on the floor to study Ben much as if he were one step narrowly removed from divinity and practically begged for the toy he was holding. 'He is a most beautiful child.'

Ben was by no means untouched by the tidal wave of almost reverential appreciation coming his way. Beaming, he bestowed the toy on his admirer. Freddy felt like a fly on the wall and tried to tell herself that she was delighted that Alula was so marvellous with children. Some time later when she had gained Ben's trust, Alula turned and opened the front door again for herself. 'Goodbye,' she said, holding Ben's hand in hers. 'Say goodbye, Ben.'

'Bye…' Ben breezed and then he suddenly pulled free of the brunette, startling her as he ran back to Freddy to demand, 'Kiss Ben!'

Swallowing hard, Freddy hugged his warm, squirming little body close. 'If he's upset, please call me. I can advise you,' she said unevenly.

With a nod that might have signified agreement, Alula walked out onto the landing. Freddy stared out at the two tough-looking men with the cropped haircuts who must have been standing out of view when the other woman had arrived. Bodyguards, she assumed, and they already had the lift open and waiting. As Ben stepped into the lift, he glanced back over his shoulder and grinned at her, patently proud of his own independence.

How trusting a confident child was, Freddy thought wretchedly as he disappeared from view and she retreated back into the apartment, almost blinded by the tears swimming in her eyes. She ought to be proud of herself. She had taught him to be confident, taken him to a playgroup from an early age and encouraged him to mix with other children as well as the nannies she had met up with from time to time.

It was the slowest, longest day of her life. She kept on trying to concentrate on how she could best explain her brief masquerade as Erica to Jaspar al-Husayn. Would he understand the shock and anxiety which had initially persuaded her into that pretence? Would he recognise and radically disapprove of the special bond between her and his nephew? And would he be reasonable? Or would he walk right back out again with Ben, shorn of any fear of her interference?

As the afternoon crept on, a tight knot began to form in Freddy's hollow stomach. She had only eaten a morsel of toast at breakfast and had not been able to face lunch. Well, Jaspar al-Husayn had said that his nanny would be spending the day with Ben and it seemed that the entire day was going to run its course. In her heart she was glad that Ben had not become upset and had not had to be brought home early, but she was also surprised. He was not accustomed to doing without her and as he got tired he usually became very clingy. But then no doubt Alula had laid on a feast of attractions to keep him distracted, or possibly Ben was being allowed to enjoy a lengthy nap.

When the bell sounded just after five, Freddy nearly broke her neck in her haste to open the door, only to fall back a step in surprise when she saw Jaspar al-Husayn poised with only his bodyguards behind him. 'Is Ben waiting in your car?' she asked. 'He must be awfully tired by now.'

'Erica…'

'Freddy,' Freddy corrected without even thinking about it, for as she stepped back automatically to allow him entrance she was too busy noting the screened darkness of his eyes, the tautness of his superb bone structure and the pronounced tension he exuded.

As his security men filed in past her Jaspar watched her peer out the door again, patently still on the watch for the little boy, who was already many thousands of miles away. He could feel her eagerness, see her distraction and he averted his attention from her with a sense of shame entirely new to him and far from welcome to a male who prided himself on his principles. Indeed, his heart sank at the task facing him: how to present an inexcusable act in terms that might even be passably acceptable. For if he did *not* contrive to placate her, the biggest scandal that had ever hit Quamar was about to break and it would be impossible to protect his people or his family from an international storm of opprobrium. She had not given legal consent to surrendering her child.

At that instant, Jaspar did not believe he would ever respect his father again. To make such an order without thought of the consequences! To issue a command like the feudal king he was in a world with media that would label him a lawless tyrant and judge Quamar as backward and uncivilised. The newspapers would inevitably expose Adil's sordid double life and cover every Quamari citizen with deep shame and dishonour. The country that Jaspar loved with every breath in his body would suffer. Right was right and wrong was wrong.

Erica or Freddy Sutton or whatever odd name she chose to call herself might be a lousy parent, but she *did* have feelings for her son. He had not initially wished to concede that, but on later appraisal he had appreciated that her every question regarding his nephew's future had been based on concern for the boy. A proper agreement had been *just* within reach. Had he not seen the defeat in her eyes and interpreted it as her sad acceptance that she was not the mother that her son deserved? But now the balance of power had changed and Jaspar was deeply conscious of that reality.

Freddy hovered as one of the bodyguards closed the front door. The hall seemed extraordinarily full of large intimidating men. Obviously, Ben wasn't coming home just yet. As the tension in the atmosphere began to tug at her awareness, a sense of foreboding assailed her. She turned to lead the way into the drawing-room, saying in an unnaturally flat voice that got nowhere near the assured tone she had hoped to strike, 'You know, Ben really should be home for his usual bedtime. That's seven, by the way.'

She turned round to face Jaspar al-Husayn, aquamarine eyes troubled, her hands knotting together in front of her.

'I have come here to ask your pardon,' he murmured in a constrained tone.

Freddy blinked, a frownline forming between her brows. That note of humility was so strikingly unexpected that she stared.

'Please sit down so that I may explain what has happened,' he continued, his grave expression and the stamp of pallor around his compressed lips betraying a tension that she could no longer pass off as the result of her own imagination.

Ben had had some kind of an accident, Freddy thought in horror, and so sick was she at that idea that her legs literally wobbled beneath her and she stumbled down onto the seat behind her. 'He's not dead...' she mumbled sickly.

'*No*. He is in good health,' Jaspar surged to assert, seemingly gaining strength from his ability to make that assurance. 'Indeed, you need have no concern at all for his physical well-being.'

'Then...then why are you asking my pardon?'

Faint dark colour scored his high cheekbones.

'This morning at half-past nine, the nanny, Alula, brought Ben to me so that we might become acquainted. It was most successful. He is a very *friendly* child,' Jaspar said with charged emphasis. 'I then went out to attend a business meeting and, when I returned late this afternoon, I received a phone call from my father...'

Freddy sat forward on the edge of the seat. 'Your...father? King Zafi?'

'Zafir...' Jaspar corrected not quite levelly, his lean brown hands clenching into fists before he lifted his proud dark head high, dark golden eyes grim. 'As soon as I had left the consulate, Alula and the individuals with her conveyed Ben to the airport. By utilising a forged Quamari passport, they were able to take your son onto the private jet awaiting them. Ben is now within an hour of landing in Quamar.'

Freddy gazed at him with wide enquiring eyes. He had wound her up too much before he had even commenced an explanation and words like 'passport' and 'consulate' were failing to connect to make sense inside her head. 'Ben is...?'

'Ben is no longer in this country,' Jaspar delivered with the curtness of stress.

No longer in this country? A frown of incomprehension drew her brows together as she struggled to come to terms with that staggering announcement. 'That can't be...'

'This covers me with shame...'

What was he talking about shame for? He had to be involved right up to his royal throat. Ben had been kidnapped by that creepy nanny! Ben had been snatched, *stolen*! Freddy's head began to whirl and her stomach to churn. A pounding pulse thumped behind her temples as she struggled to think. But it was as if her brain were suddenly wrapped in dense fog. She could not get past that first terrifying realisation that Ben might not be coming home, that all the while she had been trustingly waiting for his return he had been up in the sky in a plane that was taking him further and further away from her.

'Say goodbye...' Alula had said sweetly.

Freddy shuddered, perspiration beading her short upper lip as she wrapped her arms round herself, suddenly cold to the marrow with horror. For an instant she felt like a shocked child, incapable of imagining such cruelty. What sort of savages were these people? Jaspar al-Husayn had come here demanding her trust and she had finally given it, believing that there was no point in her even *trying* to apply for custody of Erica's son.

'You can't do it...you can't take him like that,' Freddy framed in a faraway voice, her waxen face glazed with complete shock. 'He hasn't even got his pyjamas. These things need to be planned.'

Jaspar launched himself at the decanter set sited on top of the ornate drinks cabinet, extracted a glass from within and proceeded to pour a very large brandy. It would help her, he told himself, help her through the shock. He addressed the bodyguard, poised just outside the door, in low-pitched Arabic and instructed him to call the consulate doctor. Whatever transpired, he had to contain the fallout until she had calmed down and he had had a chance to reason with her and to lie through his teeth and persuade her that really a quick and clean break was ultimately for the best. Bitter distaste and raw frustration at the prospect filled him.

Freddy wondered why he was curling her numb fingers round a bulbous brandy goblet. She had stood up without even realising it. She could see that he had spilt liquid on the top of the wood cabinet. 'I need to wipe that up,' she told him. 'It'll wreck the surface.'

'I'm sorry...I'm not used to pouring drinks.' Jaspar curved long fingers round her other hand and urged her to hold the goblet with both. The goblet was shaking.

She looked up into his darkly handsome face, marvelling

at his perfection that close, and she had not a single thought beyond that for she was still refusing to accept what he had told her. As long as she refused to believe, it wouldn't be real. For if she had to accept that it *was* real…no, no, it could not be. It was some mistake, some stupid crazy mis-understanding. He wouldn't be here saying humble words like sorry that sounded alien on his lips if there was not a explanation and if things were not soon to be sorted out, she told herself doggedly, and sipped her brandy.

The spirit raced like fire down her throat and she coughed, but then discovered that there was something cu-riously comforting about the warmth now spreading through her chilled insides and so she kept on sipping.

'We will make restitution. Anything that you want,' Jaspar murmured tautly.

'I want Ben…' Freddy did not even have to think. 'I want Ben. You're a Crown Prince. You recall that plane.'

'Though I would give much to do so, I cannot counter-mand my father's orders. He is the head of the armed forces.'

Freddy tilted her buzzing head back and blinked slowly. 'Armed forces?'

Jaspar al-Husayn loosed a ragged sigh. 'The personnel on the plane are not civilian and they will complete their mission. I am powerless to intervene but I did *try*.'

Freddy trembled. Almost everything he said was just words flying about like crazed birds dive-bombing her ears. But her mind was finally coming to grips with what he had first told her and she was being flooded with the unbearable realisation that Ben was truly gone. *Gone!* Taken without any form of agreement even from the authorities. How had she ever given her trust to such a male? How had she ever been stupid enough to let Ben leave her care for even an hour? A crime had been committed. Why had she not yet phoned the police? Letting the empty goblet fall with a crash from a nerveless hand, not even pausing to take account of the shattered glass, Freddy crunched over the shards to reach for the phone.

'What are you doing?'

And that was when it happened, when automatic pilot suddenly switched into violent reaction. As Jaspar al-Husayn lodged his big powerful frame between Freddy and the phone, which now beckoned to her much like a lifebelt to a drowning swimmer, she just exploded back into feeling and agonised awareness.

'Get out of my way!' she launched at him between gritted teeth, giving him a forceful push out of her path in a move that took him sufficiently aback to propel him sideways. 'I'm calling the police. You've broken the law. People aren't allowed to steal British citizens and I don't need a solicitor to tell me that! I'm going to create the biggest stink over this filthy business that your wretched tinpot country has ever heard! For all I know, you're planning to *kill* Ben!'

General mayhem broke out in the midst of her outburst. Suddenly his bodyguards were surrounding him as if he were being threatened by a terrorist, but not looking awfully comfortable about carrying out their duty and studying the floor with painstaking determination.

'You're such a coward...' Freddy snarled at him in disgust. 'I wish I'd punched you in the mouth!'

Hissing an outraged command in his own language, Jaspar broke through the human wall. His men shot back out of the room again at speed and closed the door behind them into the bargain. 'I am *no* coward but until you are in a state to listen to me I will not allow you to make a phone call. It pains me greatly to deny you what you have clear justification to demand but, for the moment, this appalling affair must be contained.'

As Jaspar was now between her and the phone again,

Freddy landed a kick on his shins, thinking that now he could be *genuinely* pained, and threw herself at the phone. He caught her within inches of her objective and whirled her round to face him, both hands closing over hers to restrain her. 'Though you assault me, I will not hurt you. But you *must* calm down—'

'Calm down?' Freddy shrieked, struggling wildly to escape hands that felt as strong as tempered steel. 'You can't do this to me…you can't stop me ringing the police and having you arrested as a kidnapper!'

His shimmering golden eyes clashed with hers. 'The phone lines have been disconnected.'

Freddy gazed back at him in horror. She could not use the phone? The phones were dead. Four very large men in the apartment? She was virtually a prisoner! White as a sheet at that acknowledgement, she swayed and he loosed her hands to close long, sure fingers over her upper arms and gently ease her down onto the nearest sofa.

'I mean you no harm and Ben is safe from harm as well,' Jaspar intoned, dropping down into an athletic crouch in an effort to appear unthreatening and put their eyes on a level, but he was sincerely shaken by the events of the past few minutes and the extent of her fierce protectiveness toward her child. 'I *swear* that I was not involved in any way in this disgraceful affair. I urge you to think before you act and to allow me to describe the consequences of informing the authorities. Consequences which will not only damage Ben but many other innocent people.'

CHAPTER FOUR

'MY FATHER'S phone call was brief,' Jaspar divulged, lean, powerful features taut as he lowered himself down in one sleek, fluid movement onto the sofa opposite Freddy. 'He required medical attention during the call.'

Thinking that ill health could be a very convenient excuse, Freddy was silent. Having come to the brink of hysteria, she was fighting to retain control of herself. Ben was currently out of her reach and she could not allow herself to think about that lest she break down again and lose her focus. She was recognising that the status quo had changed. Jaspar al-Husayn was afraid of what *she* might do. He had abandoned his formal royal reserve because he had no choice. The news of the disconnected phones had grounded her as nothing else could have done. He was desperate to hush up the whole matter and, in *his* desperation, she would find a way to get Ben back.

Trust and faith had been broken. No longer was she prepared to credit that Ben could find a safe and loving home in Quamar. Decent civilised people did not engage in snatching innocent children, utilising force, power and wealth to take what they wanted, regardless of the distress that would result. Her fingers bit into her palms. To think that she had been ashamed of her own small pretence! When that sin was set next to theirs, all shame evaporated and she knew that she would do whatever it took to regain Ben.

'Freddy...please listen to me.' She met the stunning dark golden eyes wholly intent on her, sensed the strong will focusing his energies on the problem. He is *very* clever, she found herself thinking, the consummate diplomat and negotiator. He will run rings round you if you let him.

Evidently unperturbed by her silence, Jaspar continued, 'After what my father has done, I *don't* expect you to have compassion for him, but Adil's death hit him very hard. From the minute he learned of your son's existence, all his thoughts have centred on him. He longs to meet his grandson. He fears that he will die before that can come about.'

He looked so concerned, sounded so incredibly sincere that Freddy wanted to hit him again. Sitting there talking, lean, bronzed face expressing just the right amount of solicitous sympathy, the rich, dark drawl full of level and reasonable appeal. It made her want to stand up and scream and attack again, smash that brilliant façade of his, for how did she know that he was even telling her the truth? How did she know that this outcome had not for some reason been planned all along? What did she really know about *their* motivations?

'I'm afraid that my admission yesterday that it would take somewhat longer than my father had hoped for me to gain custody of Ben may have caused Ben's removal without your permission,' Jaspar admitted in a tone of considerable regret.

Freddy tilted her chin. 'Talking at me won't get you anywhere. I want Ben returned and if you don't do that, you're in trouble. I bet you have diplomatic status but you're not above British law and Ben is a British citizen—'

'If this matter becomes public, Adil's family will suffer greatly. The press will dig into my late brother's private life and create a scandal that will taint every al-Husayn for many years to come.'

'Obviously someone should have had the guts to make your brother live a different life. That's not my problem,' Freddy responded without hesitation. 'I don't care about your family or your country or anything but Ben.'

'I believe that you were willing to hand him over anyway,' Jaspar countered. 'What has happened is very wrong but Ben is now in Quamar and my father will not surrender him again.'

Her small hands clenched and unclenched round each other. 'Then you take me out there to *be* with him!'

His darkly handsome features shadowed, brilliant eyes veiling. 'My father would have you deported. He would consider you a pernicious influence on the child. That investigation report on your lifestyle and your treatment of Ben appalled him.'

'What are you still sitting here for, then? You haven't got any power. You're telling me that you can do nothing, so you might as well take yourself off,' Freddy stated in a voice that, in spite of all her efforts, was starting to shake with the rising force of her emotions again. 'You have two options. Either you bring Ben back or you take me to him—'

'In time, I will be able to prevail upon my father to allow you some access to your son, but I cannot achieve that sea change overnight,' Jaspar reasoned, spreading lean brown hands in a graceful motion of appeal that utterly fascinated her.

He had been tutored in body language, she thought bitterly. How to act open and honest and human. But he needn't think she was being taken in…behind those eyes he was out-thinking and out-talking her, endeavouring to make her accept that what had happened could not be changed for the present, but that he would work on her behalf to reason with his tyrannical old father.

'I don't believe anything you say. I want Ben. I'll go to the police, and if the police don't listen because you're royal and powerful and rich, I'll go to the newspapers and you had *better* believe that the press will listen!' Freddy warned him between chattering teeth for she was breaking up inside herself, her hard-won composure refusing to hold up any longer for every time she said Ben's name she was engulfed in pain.

'Do you think that your son will some day thank you for revealing that you went to bed with his father solely to enrich yourself? Are you prepared to tell the world that you conceived a child only for profit and neglected him?'

Her aquamarine eyes focused on him in shaken horror. She shut her eyes tight. She was trying so hard not to think of how Ben's day must have gone. He would have enjoyed meeting Jaspar. The airport and the plane would probably have been a thrill, but during the long flight his confidence would've begun to dip for too many strange events would have been forced on him in too short a space of time. He would have begun asking for her, needing contact with familiar faces and surroundings to feel safe. As time went on, he would've become increasingly bewildered and unhappy because he was only a baby and so far his life had taught him that what he wanted, be it food, cuddles or Freddy, he would always receive. When she failed to appear, he would be frightened and he would cry…and was that creepy nanny, Alula, likely to be much consolation?

Silent tears were trickling down Freddy's face. Momentarily Jaspar shut his own eyes. As she suddenly twisted and flung herself down into the tumbled cushions as if she felt forced to try and hide her grief from him, he could stand the distance between them no longer.

'I swear on my honour something will be done, no matter what it takes,' he breathed, sinking down on the sofa to one side of her shaking body to smooth her hair back from her brow in an almost awkward movement.

'Go away…you bastard!' Freddy sobbed brokenly and wept all the harder.

The dam-burst of distress she had fought to contain for so long could be contained no longer.

'Freddy…'

'Your sick father has just taken a two-year-old on a whim and what's g-going to happen when he loses interest in Ben or he dies? Who's likely to want Ben after there's been a ghastly scandal and all your hateful family have suffered because of him?' Freddy condemned on another wave of gasping sobs.

Jaspar found himself facing an angle he had not yet considered because his whole being was bent on persuading her to remain silent. He swore under his breath and at that point the consulate doctor crept in and bowed very low.

Freddy could not stop crying. All she could think about was Ben's distress and her own complete inability to help him. No matter how big a fuss she might make, it was unlikely to bring Ben home. Kings did not grovel to public opinion beyond their borders, not an old tyrant capable of having his grandson snatched, anyway. She suspected that King Zafir was as stubborn as a pig and would go to his deathbed without admitting that he had done wrong. Why had she thought she had power, for the power to threaten was *not* enough, was it? Not if it ultimately damaged Ben and his prospects in Quamar.

How could she gain power in such a situation? Freddy wondered frantically. How could she go out to Quamar and be there for Ben without being threatened with deportation? If only she were someone important, someone who had status, someone who could not be written off as a nobody and ignored and refused entry to their precious country! And then in a flash it came to her.

She felt the slight prick of the injection in her arm but was much too deep in her desperate ruminations to pay proper heed. It was insane but hadn't Jaspar offered her, 'Anything that you want' and didn't she have him over a barrel? But she needed to protect herself too, didn't she? The price of her silence would be a wedding ring. He could marry her…secretly, put her in a veil or something and smuggle her into Quamar. Surely that wouldn't be beyond his power? She could look after Ben then and live in some rural, underpopulated spot until the old king had got fed up with his two-year-old grandson or died. Then Jaspar could divorce her and she could bring Ben home again. Nobody need ever know.

'You could marry me…' Freddy said dizzily, opening eyes with dilated pupils and registering that she was lying on her back looking up at Jaspar without any recollection of having moved.

Stunning golden eyes enhanced by spiky ebony lashes widened as they gazed down into hers with transfixed attention.

'Secretly…' Freddy added, sounding rather smug and feeling oddly euphoric, noting that the ceiling above was shiny and reflective without wondering why. 'Hide me. I'd keep quiet and look after Ben and then when the time's right, you divorce me.'

Jaspar watched her big aquamarine eyes drift closed and a vague sphinx-like smile curve her lush mouth. He emerged from the lift and tightened his hold on her as he strode out to the waiting limousine. She had been given a very mild sedative yet her mind was wandering. The doctor had been unhappy when Jaspar had admitted administering brandy, but he had assumed a woman who threw wild drunken parties on a regular basis would require a *large* brandy to feel any beneficial soothing effects. Perhaps she was hallucinating.

Marry her in secret and hide her? She had an incredibly colourful imagination. In the rear of the limo, he cradled her limp body. He had not liked that smile. She could not demand such an act of insanity and personal sacrifice from him. Every nerve fibre rebelled at the mere mention of his marrying a woman of her character and reputation. A drunken and promiscuous gold-digger...yet, in spite of all those men, she still tried to kiss with her mouth sealed shut like a teeny-bopper who didn't know any better.

Freddy wakened slowly, stretching in glorious comfort before opening her sleepy eyes.

But it only took one look at her unfamiliar surroundings for her to thrust herself up against the pillows in shaken disconcertion. Dim dawn light was filtering through a chink in the curtains. Scanning the grand bedroom, she glanced down in equal confusion at the nightdress she wore, an opulent blue satin and lace affair with a low neck. A slight sound made her jerk in dismay and she was even more unnerved by the sight of the tall dark shape unfolding from a chair in a shadowy corner. A muffled gasp of fright escaped her.

'It is only I...' Jaspar al-Husayn's familiar drawl sounded.

'Where on earth am I?' Freddy demanded, sufficiently reassured to give vent to her angry bewilderment.

He touched a wall switch and the tall lamps on either side of the bed came on. Pools of soft light illuminated the taut set of his bronzed features and the brightness of his incisive gaze, but also delineated the strained line of his sculpted mouth and the shadow of dark stubble now roughening his strong jawline. 'You're in the Consulate of Quamar. To be within reach of a secure phone line, I had to return here last night and I couldn't leave you alone in the state that you were in.'

Still attempting to come to terms with having woken up in a totally strange environment, Freddy protested. 'But I've been asleep for hours. I remember someone giving me an injection—'

'A doctor and it was a very mild sedative,' Jaspar qualified in the same maddeningly even tone. 'Please do not accuse me of having kidnapped you as well. I could not abandon you as you were, nor could I remain in that apartment—'

'Ben…' Momentarily, Freddy was rocked by the memory of the previous day's events and the pain of recollection pierced her deep. 'Have you heard anything yet?'

Jaspar straightened his wide shoulders. 'That the flight landed safely and that Ben was put straight to bed when he arrived at the palace. He's fine.'

On the brink of arguing with that optimistic statement, Freddy became conscious of the manner in which his lion-gold gaze was resting on her. The silence hummed. Her mouth ran dry, her pulses quickening. Within the satin bodice, her breasts stirred, making her embarrassingly aware not only of the straining sensitivity of her nipples, but also that she was distinctly underdressed. Her cheeks flaming, Freddy yanked the sheet clumsily higher and anchored it beneath her arms. 'Who put me to bed?'

'The maids.'

'And what are you doing in here?'

'I knew you would be frightened when you woke up in a strange place. Do you remember what you suggested to me last night?' Jaspar enquired softly, poised at the foot of the bed, brilliant golden eyes intent on her.

Freddy lost colour. So it had not been a crazy dream that she had told him he ought to marry her to get her into Quamar and a position where she could be reunited with Ben. She could see that he was expecting her to be embarrassed but she found herself lifting her chin, something odd and unfamiliar but decidedly aggressive powering her. 'Perfectly.'

'But it could only have been the brandy talking. To demand that I should marry you? What could be more ridiculous?' Jaspar asked, smooth as silk.

Her taut fingers dug into the sheet she was clutching. 'A

nasty old tyrant of a king kidnapping his grandson with army personnel? Them acting like a bunch of terrorists on foreign soil? Your late brother's taste for sleazy sex on the ocean waves? Well, perhaps not ridiculous but, let's face it, royal you may be...but where your family's concerned, you've got nothing to be proud of. And certainly no good reason to think you're one bit better than I am!'

Jaspar was outraged by her abuse of his family. Paling as though she had struck him, he flung his proud dark head back, a current of rage unlike anything he had ever experienced shooting up through his lean, powerful frame. In all his life he had never had to withstand such an attack and the unhappy grains of truth within the content only further inflamed him. Only hours earlier, he had had a violent argument with his father on the phone on *her* behalf, the father whom he had been brought up to respect as both sovereign and parent, the father whose will he had been taught never ever to question.

But there she sat unafraid and defying him, like some Lorelei on the rocks, draped in a wild tangle of blonde curls, a siren in human form but pure cutting steel beneath the alluring femininity. And he promised himself then that, no matter what happened or what it cost him, there would be a reckoning for her attempt to soil him with the same dirt that clung to her.

Freddy raised an unsteady hand to her pounding brow. She was shocked at what she had thrown at him, amazed that such venom had come so readily to her usually gentle tongue. Jaspar might be the unacceptable face of the al-Husayn royal family, every one of whom she now loathed sight unseen, but she *did* recognise that he had drawn the short straw. His brother, Adil, had got off scot-free with his excesses and his sick father was pretty much untouchable, for who was likely to tell home truths to an absolute monarch, who enjoyed unfettered power?

'Are you telling me that the matrimonial proposition was serious?' Jaspar demanded, his wrathful incredulity unconcealed.

Freddy froze. She had been half out of her mind with grief when she had come up with that wild idea. Thinking of it afresh, she still saw it as a wild idea, but *not* necessarily the wrong idea if it was her only hope of influencing events and reclaiming Ben from what she now viewed as the lawless hell-hole of Quamar. Right now, she knew that she had the most power that she would ever have. He did not want the police or the press to get wind of what had happened, but he could not prevent her from informing them.

'Unless you can come up with something better than you offered me last night,' Freddy muttered tightly. 'Yes, I was serious. I want Ben home. But, failing that, I want to be with him.'

'I refuse to marry you,' Jaspar growled. 'You're trying to blackmail me—'

Freddy considered that angle and then nodded with an apologetic light in her anxious aquamarine eyes. 'Yes, I suppose I am, but I'm only concerned with Ben's happiness and I can't trust your promises—'

Jaspar shot her a scorching look of raw incredulity. 'Yet you are willing to *marry* me?'

'I don't think even your father could get away with throwing me out of the country if I was your wife,' Freddy pointed out. 'After all, if he did that, I would have an even bigger story to tell the newspapers when I came home, so the need to keep me quiet and reasonably content would be an ongoing necessity.'

'Oh, I could do that...I could do that easily,' Jaspar murmured throatily, his rich, dark drawl rousing a curious little twist of heat deep in her pelvis as he braced lean brown hands on the high footboard of the antique bed.

As the silence pulsed like the quiet before a volcanic eruption, Freddy stared into vibrant golden eyes. Dizzy and enervated, she opened her mouth so that the tip of her tongue could sneak out to moisten her dry lips. She watched his gaze lower there and her lips tingled in response as she struggled to recapture her focus. 'Marriage would protect me…'

'Would it?' Jaspar prompted, indolent in tone as a prowling jungle cat.

'Nobody need ever know and you would just go on with your life as if I didn't exist. It would only be a sign of good faith on your part…that's all.'

'A sign of good faith,' Jaspar ground out. 'And this you truly demand of me? It *is* blackmail…have you no shame?'

'Not where Ben's concerned.' Freddy cast her eyes down because she refused to retreat from what she saw as her only hope of seeing Ben again.

Unimpressed by the evident emotional pang now assailing her, Jaspar withdrew his hands from the footboard to curl them into fists of restraint. 'OK…since shame doesn't come into this equation—how much cash do you want to keep this whole affair quiet?'

Freddy's head came up in shock and she gave him a look of horror. 'Ben isn't for sale. How can you even *suggest* that I would accept money from you?'

Jaspar backed off to the wall, no longer trusting himself that close to his tormentor. 'You took it from Adil—'

Freddy flushed. 'That was different.'

'But with me…it's marriage or nothing, right?' Jaspar's dark drawl was raw-edged as he moved with fluid grace round to the side of the bed.

'All I want is access to Ben. Don't forget that option,' Freddy hurried to remind him, for really he was going on as though marrying him might be her sole objective and it was becoming rather embarrassing.

Jaspar came down on the bed so slowly she was mesmerised into the belief that he actually wasn't doing what he was doing. 'And what do you think I'm going to get out of this deal?'

Freddy gazed at him with huge aquamarine eyes and stopped breathing like a fawn trying to blend into woodland, scared that a sudden movement might provoke the hunter. And that was exactly how she felt. That close to Jaspar al-Hussayn, she was on the edge of such an electrifying charge of fevered anticipation that she could barely think straight, but she could feel the danger all right.

'You think I want you,' Jaspar murmured thickly.

''Course I don't,' Freddy mumbled, feeling the buzz in the air, the enervating high of awareness of his virile masculinity that close. But while even the most basic caution urged retreat, she did not move a muscle.

'You *know* I do.'

Freddy's heart skipped a beat in sheer shock. *He* wanted *her*? She studied him with fascination, helplessly thrilled by that admission. He was sober. He didn't look like he was about to unload the story of how his last girlfriend had made his life a living hell either. He found her attractive? A guy who looked like her every fantasy come true actually found her attractive. 'You do…*honestly*?' she prompted breathlessly, leaning forward, keen to hear him tell her that all over again.

Jaspar reached out and slowly laced long brown fingers into the tumbling fall of blonde waves and drew her down against the pillows. In shock at that bold move, her heartbeat hit earthquake mode and she opened her mouth to protest but somehow said nothing. Locked to that scorching golden gaze, she was mesmerised, deliciously aware of every fibre of her own feminine body. An almost painful ache stirred low in her stomach, making her shiver.

He took her mouth in an exploratory foray and she felt

as if she were flying, only not fast enough, and seemingly of their own volition her hands rose and her fingers dug into his silky black hair, dragging him down to her. She felt engulfed by him then, the lean, hard weight and heat and strength of him, and excitement raced through her like a shooting star. His tongue plunged into the tender interior of her mouth and she gasped, her spine arching as he cupped her breast, teased the distended pink nipple with expert fingers. A moan was torn from deep in her throat. Sensation flooded her in a wave of response so strong, it brought her crashing back to awareness.

As she jerked, aquamarine eyes flying wide, Jaspar was already snaking back from her to snatch up the bedside phone. Freddy had never been more mortified in her life and was very grateful that he was paying attention only to his call. Feverishly flushed and overheated, she gazed down in dismay at the gaping neckline, the sight of her own bare breast crowned by a wanton peak. Hurriedly covering herself, she hauled the sheet up to her chin, shut her eyes tight and snatched in a ragged breath.

Jaspar was talking in his own language, dark drawl cool, clipped and level. She cringed beneath the sheet, rolled over, pushed her burning face into the pillow. There was just no excuse for her behaviour. She hardly knew him, nor was she in the habit of rolling about beds and allowing such liberties. How that passion had erupted in the midst of what had been a virtual argument, she had no idea, but she was seriously shaken by her own behaviour.

'We'll get married tomorrow morning.'

Having tensed at the sound of him tossing down the phone, Freddy blinked, hearing literally on full alert. Slowly she raised her head, unable to immediately absorb that startling announcement, couched in the coldest of tones. *'Tomorrow?'*

'Here within the consulate, the laws of my own country

prevail. The ceremony must take place as soon as possible because I want to be back in Quamar by tomorrow evening.' Lean, powerful face grim, Jaspar surveyed her with glittering golden eyes that had the oddest chilling effect on her.

'You're…you're actually prepared to go through with this and marry me?' Ironically, Freddy was shattered by her own victory.

'As you are well aware, I have little choice. I must pay the price of your silence.'

And then *she* would pay the price for her blackmail and the greed and ambition which had prompted such a preposterous demand, Jaspar reflected with grim satisfaction. By marrying him, she would become a Quamari citizen and, as a member of the royal family, much less fortunate than the rest of the populace in terms of personal freedom. Marooned in the desert, she would find precious little to amuse her, but then he was thinking more of his *own* amusement. Presumably, her son would also benefit from her presence until he had forged other relationships. Once that feat had been achieved and his nephew seemed secure and content, Jaspar planned to dispense with her services. By that stage, he would probably be pretty tired of her in any case.

As he studied her with veiled eyes a faint smile curved his handsome mouth. She was as luscious as a peach and he was entranced by the air of utter innocence that she had perfected. Had he not known what he did know about her shallow, avaricious nature, he might even have been taken in, just as the night before he had been genuinely disturbed by her apparent anguish at being parted from her son. But he need have no finer sensibilities about teaching her a lesson.

Stealing a glance at him, her eyes full of guilty discomfiture, Freddy wondered what he had found to smile about, for she could not have raised a smile should her life have depended on it. *The price of your silence*. He was prepared to meet her demand to save his precious family from public embarrassment. But those words, those cold and unforgiving words so redolent of blackmail shamed her. However, it was Ben she was concerned about, *only* Ben, and he would eventually recognise that, wouldn't he?

'All I care about is Ben…' Freddy muttered almost pleadingly.

'I'll order breakfast for you. I suggest that you return to your apartment and pack. I'll send a car to pick you up tomorrow at eight,' Jaspar informed her.

'You can't possibly go through with marrying him…' Ruth Coulter said with an amount of disbelief that unnerved Freddy that evening.

Freddy bent her blonde head even lower over the case she was packing and suppressed a groan. Ruth had come over to the apartment as soon as Freddy had called her. Although aghast at the manner in which the al-Husayn family had taken possession of Ben, she was very much more shocked by Freddy's solution to that crisis.

'It's the only way I can get to see Ben and have some influence over what happens to him out there,' Freddy muttered defensively.

'For goodness' sake…by forcing the Crown Prince to make you his wife?'

'Only on paper. I mean, it's going to be a secret, nobody's ever likely to know about it. But if I hadn't played that card, there was no way I was *ever* going to get into Quamar!' Freddy protested feelingly. 'The marriage bit is only to ensure that Jaspar has good reason to help me and he wasn't planning to help me otherwise, just fob me off with vague promises. Really, the marriage angle will be very short-lived—'

'How?'

Freddy breathed in deep. 'Well, Ben's grandfather will probably lose interest in him and of course by that stage I'll have come clean about who I am and then I'd be able to bring Ben home...*or*...' Freddy trailed out the word in desperation as the older woman's frown simply deepened. '...or maybe, there'll be a couple...as Jaspar suggested...who want to make Ben their son. If that happens, I swear that I'll accept the situation and bow out.'

'If you'd told the Crown Prince that you were only Erica's cousin and Ben's nanny at the beginning, would any of this have even happened?' Ruth demanded. 'You might well have found yourself invited out to Quamar *with* Ben!'

Freddy stiffened. 'I don't think so. He already had a nanny organised and he talked about a clean break being the best thing for Ben, which just shows how much *he* knows about children!'

'You haven't thought this through,' the older woman warned her in growing frustration. 'All you're thinking about is Ben.'

'Yes,' Freddy affirmed. 'But it's my job to look out for him because there's nobody else to do it. The least I can do is be there for him until he doesn't need me any more.'

'I've never seen you like this before. If only Erica had left a will.' Ruth sighed, studying the younger woman's unusually set and stubborn expression. 'I'm surprised she didn't because she said she was planning to have one drawn up.'

'She also said she'd have to find a gorgeous solicitor first.' A sad smile curved Freddy's lips at that recollection. 'But a will wouldn't have changed this situation.'

'It might well have done. Erica may not have been a good mother but she *did* recognise that you were,' Ruth replied thoughtfully.

Paying little heed to that opinion, Freddy closed her suitcase and hauled it out to the hall to sit beside the other case she had already packed for Ben.

'Freddy...you simply *can't* blackmail Ben's uncle into marrying you,' Ruth emphasised even more forcefully. 'A man who despises you won't help you and may even go out of his way to punish you for putting him in an impossible position. Let me go and talk to him and tell him who you really are...'

On the drive to the Consulate of Quamar early the following morning, Freddy was still thinking back with regret to that conversation, for she was more used to taking Ruth's advice than flying in the face of it. But admitting her real identity was too dangerous and she was not prepared to risk sacrificing any prospect of seeing Ben again. Ben needed her and whatever it took she would go to him.

Although she had hoped that the blue three-piece designer suit she wore would make her feel more confident, she was uncomfortable in such finery. The skirt felt too short and neat fitting for relaxation and she felt too bare in the thin strappy top she wore below the neat little jacket. Always generous, Erica had often bought Freddy identical outfits to those she had worn herself, but Freddy had only ever worn them to please on an occasional basis. The contrast between Erica's extreme slenderness and her own greater abundance in the same garments had always been too painful a reminder to Freddy of her own failings.

But then from adolescence on, people had often made thoughtless comparisons between the two girls, for Erica had neither gone through the embarrassing puppy-fat stage which had once tormented Freddy, nor suffered from tongue-tied shyness in the company of others. Frequent criticism from her father for her awkwardness had caused Freddy's self-esteem to sink low and she had taken refuge in sweatshirts and trousers, determined not to compete in any way with Erica's ultra-feminine appearance.

When Freddy was fifteen, Erica had persuaded one of her friends to invite Freddy out on a date. Unaware that her cousin had been busy behind the scenes, Freddy had been thrilled. Her pleasure, however, had been short-lived. Returning from the cloakroom after seeing the film that evening, she had heard her date saying to a mate, ''Course, I *don't* fancy her! Erica gave me twenty quid to take her out.'

Freddy had wept long and hard that night but she had never told Erica that she had found out the truth. And when, four years later, Erica had stolen Freddy's first serious boyfriend while home on a weekend visit, Freddy had been a really good sport about it. After all, Steve had been very attractive and Freddy had felt that it had been all too good to be true from the minute he'd shown an interest in her.

'I'm sorry,' Erica had groaned guiltily on the phone the following week. 'I was only testing him out for you.'

'Steve wasn't important to me,' Freddy had insisted valiantly, wiping her streaming swollen eyes dry with her sleeve, fighting to retain a little dignity after having been dumped like a hot potato.

And within a couple of years of that experience Freddy had stopped actively trying to attract the opposite sex and based her social life on interest shared solely with female friends. Life had seemed very much smoother and simpler. Joking that when a man approached her he only wanted a sympathetic shoulder to cry on had become second nature to her. But staying home in recent years had also become a necessity with Erica away so much and Freddy reluctant to hire a babysitter.

If only she hadn't kissed Jaspar, Freddy reflected in guilty discomfiture. Not just once but twice and what an idiot she had made of herself! Only, *he* didn't know that, though, did he? He probably just thought she was as loose as her apparent reputation, which was of some comfort. But, nonetheless, that unfortunate intimacy brought in a more personal and embarrassing dimension and made maintaining a dignified distance more difficult. Well, there would be no more nonsense in that line, she told herself squarely.

At the consulate, Freddy was shown into a room which contained two grave-faced men, who introduced themselves as lawyers. She was totally taken aback and intimidated by that development and within minutes was tied in knots of shamefaced mortification while she wondered how much they knew about the situation between herself and Jaspar. A document described as a marriage and confidentiality contract was set in front of her.

With an unsteady hand and burning cheeks, Freddy made a play of glancing through the document, which stretched to forty-three pages of clauses and sub-clauses couched in almost impenetrable legalese. Nowhere could she see a mention of Ben. Reassured, she sighed, recognising that it had been foolish of her not to expect such a demand. Evidently having expected some argument, her companions looked rather nonplussed.

For a while she was left alone in the room. Then Jaspar arrived, accompanied by the lawyers and an imposing white-bearded clergyman wearing a long robe. Colliding with Jaspar's grim dark eyes, Freddy paled. For the first time, she acknowledged that entering a marriage on such terms went against everything she had ever been brought up to respect. Her tummy twisted with guilt and unease and she averted her attention from him. Yet still his image and the impression he made on her remained stamped in her mind's eye; the taut gravity of his lean, handsome features, his commanding height and breadth in a tailored light grey suit, his striking self-command in a challenging situation.

It was, somewhat to Freddy's surprise, a Christian ceremony, which made her feel even worse. At the end of it, nothing was said. Their companions filed back out again, leaving her alone with Jaspar.

'Are you satisfied now?' he breathed almost indolently.

Freddy gave him a harried nod. 'This wouldn't have happened if you'd given me another option,' she muttered uncomfortably.

Jaspar appraised her with glittering eyes the colour of pure gold. Without the smallest warning, he reached for her with complete cool and pulled her close, one lean hand curving to her hip in the most disconcertingly intimate fashion. Freddy reddened and attempted to step back, but he held her fast.

'What are you doing?'

'Handling the merchandise I just acquired,' Jaspar murmured softly.

'I beg your pardon?' Freddy gasped.

'I don't like your hair up like that.' Long fingers swooped up to the clip holding her hair tight to the back of her skull and tossed it away so that a tangled thicket of pale blonde curls descended *en masse* to her shoulders.

'Do you really think that I don't plan to profit in some way from this deal too?' Jaspar surveyed her bewildered and beautiful face with hard amusement and freed her when she least expected it, leaving her standing there trembling and disconcerted.

'What are you talking about?' Freddy stooped to retrieve her hair clip with as much defiance as she could muster and, throwing back her head, she wound her hair up into a twisted coil, restoring it to order.

'You'll find out. By the way, you got the ring but you didn't acquire a title. Only my father can make you a princess and, if I were you, I wouldn't hold my breath on that score.'

'What would I want to be a princess for?' Freddy snapped, that angle not even having occurred to her.

'By the time our paths separate, you might just feel that you've earned the privilege,' Jaspar quipped, smooth as silk.

He was trying to scare her out of flying back to Quamar with him, Freddy decided, and her chin came up. One thing he needed to learn about her, she thought, she was no quitter. As far as she was concerned, that marriage ceremony had brought her one giant step closer to Ben and that was all that need concern her.

CHAPTER FIVE

SECURE in the knowledge that she would soon see Ben, Freddy assumed that her stress level would return to normal.

However, the sight of the entire flight crew dropping to their knees to greet Jaspar when they boarded the private jet shook Freddy a great deal. Until that moment, his royal status had not seemed quite real to her, but the solemn respect he commanded was striking. The luxurious interior of the jet and a main cabin the size of her late cousin's drawing-room impressed her to death. Settled in a leather reclining seat and besieged with magazines, refreshments and an array of movies by the attendants, she felt as though she were a lottery winner on the holiday of a lifetime.

As the flight progressed Freddy found herself watching Jaspar almost continually. The longer she spent in his radius, the more he fascinated her. While he worked on his notebook computer, she noted the extraordinary length of his lush ebony lashes, the smooth, sculpted line of his high cheekbones, the narrow-boned perfection of his nose and the passionate curve of that mobile mouth.

He was drop-dead gorgeous and when he talked on his satellite phone, chatting first in French and later in Spanish with easy fluency, and she caught a glimpse of his vibrant dark golden eyes alive with intelligence and energy, her attention was engaged even more.

She watched him move a lean hand in fluid expressiveness, proud dark head angled to one side. Then he shot a glance in her direction and caught her staring. She felt the blood rise beneath her fair skin, the tight clenching sensa-

tion low in her pelvis, the surge of instantaneous heat that
followed, but was powerless to control her own physical
response. In haste, she wrenched her dismayed gaze from
the hard grip of his, her heart racing frantically fast.

Why did she have to be so wretchedly, pointlessly at-
tracted to him? Freddy's teeth gritted. She was furious with
herself and mortified. Why did she have to act like a silly
daydreaming schoolkid around him? Was she suddenly
turning into a sex-starved woman desperate for a man?
Assailed by that lowering suspicion, she felt her colour rise
even higher. How often had Ruth chided her for steering
clear of men? But then, it was all very well for Ruth to
talk, but times had changed in the dating game. Freddy did
not believe in casual sex but, when she had dated, she had
been put on the spot time and time again, forced to defend
her views and laughed at and scorned on more than one
occasion.

Jaspar sank back down into his seat, stretched out in one
long, measured movement and contemplated his blushing
bride with cynical amusement. Had she been his acknowledged wife, he would have taken her to the big bed in the
main sleeping compartment and eased the ache of his throbbing sex without hesitation, for rarely had he received a
more blatant unspoken invitation. However, discretion was
the name of the game and such a flagrant act would be
unwise. Many of his people would soon be aware that he
was keeping a woman in his desert palace for gossip was
food and drink to the Quamaris. But what he did not flaunt
would be acceptable as long as he still appeared to be single.

In addition, the rumour of her existence would serve to
keep Sabirah at bay, Jaspar mused, a rather cruel light
gleaming in his reflective gaze. Sabirah, whom he had once
hoped to marry. Sabirah, whom he had adored with passionate idealism and who had appeared to return his feel-

ings right up until the moment that Adil's wandering eye had fallen on her. Ambition had triumphed. Though she had barely been half his brother's age, Sabirah had disdained the younger son and had chosen to become the heir to the throne's third wife. But since Adil's untimely death Sabirah had been behaving with dangerous impropriety.

Was he for ever condemned to pay for his elder brother's sins? Jaspar wondered with sudden fierce bitterness. Here he was with yet another of Adil's cast-offs, forced to link his proud name with that of a female unfit to breathe the same air as the women in his family, a heartless gold-digger who had not batted an eyelash at the news that the father of her child was dead. Lean, powerful face taut, he surveyed her. She had spirit, though. He *liked* women with spirit. If he had to tell the staff to destroy every hair ornament in the Anhara, she would wear that glorious blonde mane loose for his pleasure. The prospect of spreading her across his bed and driving her wild with desire filled him with more hungry impatience than he had felt in a long time. Adil might have bought her favours but *he* would be the one who truly possessed her.

As the jet juddered to a final halt and the steps were rushed to the exit door, Freddy sat very stiff in her leather seat, staring out at the superb ultra-modern airport. Never before had she been in company with a male so polished at simply ignoring her existence. True, Jaspar seemed to be an exceptionally busy male, but surely a little casual conversation would not have killed him?

She felt extremely foolish when he moved to disembark without even looking in her direction. Rushing to catch up with him, she whispered urgently, 'Have you a veil or something so that I can cover myself up?'

'Were you hoping for one?' Over one broad shoulder, Jaspar slanted her a gleaming golden glance of mockery.

'Sorry. A veil would cause more of a sensation than your face. Quamari women don't shroud themselves because we are not Muslim. This *is* a Christian country.'

Freddy went scarlet at that unexpected revelation and wished she had had the opportunity to learn more about the country that was to be her home for at least the next few weeks. It was hot and nervous tension made her feel even more flustered. It was not a pleasant surprise either when Jaspar headed for the helicopter a few yards away instead of continuing on towards the airport building.

'We're travelling on from here?'

'Yes.' While the pilot was bowing low to the ground, Jaspar closed strong hands round her waist and lifted her up into the helicopter.

Freddy did up the seat belt with anxious hands. 'When will I *see*—?'

'I hope to bring him home with me late this evening but you will have to practise patience,' Jaspar imparted. 'I must speak to my father first'

'But what if he says no?' Freddy prompted fearfully.

Jaspar flashed her an exasperated look. Was she downright stupid or something? Of course, his father would say *no*! But the announcement that he had married Ben's mother would take precedence at that meeting for he would not lie to his father. Such a secret could not be kept from the older man and, unless he was very much mistaken, his father would immediately attempt to have the marriage set aside on the grounds that it had taken place without his permission. A divorce would not be necessary. Nor would it be necessary to tell his bride that within the space of weeks, and without her consent, she would almost inevitably be dispossessed of him again.

The craft rose into the air and tilted into a turn, churning up Freddy's stomach with a panoramic view of the city skyscrapers beyond the airport. As the helicopter flew out over the desert, she stared out initially in dismay at the emptiness. But almost as soon she began to see with a keener eye and note the strange rock formations and the green valleys scattered with flat-roofed houses before the rippling sand in shades of ochre and cinnamon and gold took over again for miles.

It was a relief to step out onto solid ground again.

'This is the Anhara, my private home,' Jaspar murmured.

Standing on the edge of the heli-pad, Freddy gazed in wonderment at the lush gardens full of mature trees and colourful shrubs that stretched as far as the eye could see. No building was even visible. 'What a beautiful place.'

'It was once a Moorish fortress. I had the gardens restored some years ago.' Jaspar's strong jawline clenched as he recalled why.

A paved almost secret path led below the trees to a glorious arched entrance built of ancient stone and etched with intricate carving. With the sensation that she had wandered into another world and one of pure enchantment, Freddy followed in his wake, barely noticing the rank of servants on their knees, more interested in the fabulous interior that just shrieked antiquity. She was going to live in this wonderful building? My goodness, she ought to be paying him for the privilege!

'Freddy…' Waiting for her to negotiate the magnificent stone staircase, Jaspar extended an impatient hand to hurry her on. A sudden smile flashed across his bronzed features as he watched her caress the worn carved balustrade with gentle fingers, her awestruck appreciation touching him for he took his surroundings entirely for granted. But then a lesson in good taste would do her no harm. He almost shuddered at the memory of her over-gilded and flashy apartment.

Freddy looked up into that smile and was as dazzled as if Jaspar had turned a spotlight on her in darkness. Shaken and dizzy, she felt the warmth of his hand close over hers and she trembled, the breath tripping in her throat, her mouth running dry. His eyes roved over her with an intensity that sent a wicked shard of excitement flaring through her.

Jaspar removed the hair clip with pronounced care for the second time in two days, flung it aside with an arrogant hand. 'Now I will take you to my bed and pleasure you.'

Her aquamarine eyes widened in direct proportion to her shock. It was one thing looking, another thing for her to be dreaming in that line, but altogether something else again for him to threaten to turn safe if risqué fantasy into very dangerous reality. 'I b-beg—?'

'Yes, you *will*,' Jaspar husked in throaty and undeniable promise, swooping down to sweep her off her startled feet and lift her into his arms before she had the slightest conception of what he was doing.

'Put me down this minute!' Freddy spluttered.

'It's safe to drop the blushing *ingénue* act now,' Jaspar delivered with amused superiority as he strode towards the double doors set below an arch across the vast upper landing. 'Before it becomes a bore.'

'A...bore?' Freddy whispered shakily.

'I prefer an honest passion in my women,' Jaspar divulged in the tone of one set on educating. 'You're hot as hell for me and I for you—'

'No, I'm not!' Freddy slung at him a full octave higher as he shouldered his way through one of the doors with complete cool. 'You've got the wrong idea—'

'I do hope not,' Jaspar murmured in a sizzling undertone that shimmied down her spine like a storm warning of sensual threat.

But as he crossed the anteroom into the spacious bedroom beyond, Freddy was quite incapable of responding for the most extraordinary sight had seized her attention and closed up her vocal cords simultaneously. A stark naked and very beautiful brunette was reclining across the vast bed like some seductive houri in an oil painting, every stunning angle of her exquisite body posed to attract and about three feet of silken hair draped over one shoulder to fall into an elaborate coil down onto the pale sheet.

Appalled by all that rampant nudity on display, Freddy flushed scarlet. Jaspar froze, uttered what sounded like a stifled oath and then literally dumped Freddy down onto the chaise longue just over the threshold. Gaping, Freddy watched as the now infuriated brunette rose up on her knees and let out a screech that would have shattered glass. Beestung red lips no longer arranged in a sensual smile, slanted dark eyes flashing with incredulous fury, the female flew off the bed like a tigress ready to claw.

Jaspar, who was strikingly pale, loosed a volley of freezing Arabic and snatched up the bedspread to fling it at the woman.

'Excuse me...' he murmured with unearthly cool to Freddy, striding back out of the room again.

'Who are you?' the brunette shrieked at Freddy, struggling to wrap the spread round her lissom curves. 'Jaspar spoke to you in English. You foreign slut!'

Aghast, Freddy shrank her shoulders in and averted her attention, thinking that her companion really shouldn't be hurling insults of that nature at anybody else. Who was she? His discarded mistress? My goodness, he had had no compunction about rejecting her, had he? A trio of female servants rushed in and began to urge the woman from the room. Before she got out of earshot, she was sobbing noisily.

At last, silence fell. Freddy snatched in a shaken breath as the door onto the landing thudded shut again and steps sounded on the tiled floor of the anteroom. Well, he had said women threw themselves at him, but she had not realised he'd meant it quite so literally, and what on earth he could possibly want with *her* when that *femme fatale* had been lying in eager wait for him, she could not begin to imagine.

'Now where were we...?' Jaspar enquired lazily.

Shattered by that proof of his indestructible self-assurance, Freddy glanced up at him in frank wonderment. 'We weren't anywhere,' she mumbled. 'Nor are we going to be.'

'This is our wedding night.' His brilliant tawny eyes shimmied over her in the most familiar fashion imaginable and left her feeling hugely self-conscious. 'You're my wife and I intend to enjoy you.'

Aquamarine eyes wide, Freddy stared back at him, bereft of words for she could see that he was serious. '*Enjoy* you.' It was a very revealing phrase. One enjoyed a meal, a sport, an experience. Where she came from, the average male did not talk about *enjoying* a woman as though her body were a service on offer. But then she was not in England now, she was in Quamar and she did not think his usually wonderful grasp of English was at fault. She believed that that choice of words had been quite deliberate.

'Surprised?' Jaspar elevated a winged ebony brow, a derisive light in his incisive gaze. 'I hardly think so. Forcing me to marry you was not the act of a sensitive woman. Though you knew that I was solely concerned with your son's well-being and that I had not been involved in his removal from London, you insisted that I go through with that mockery of a ceremony. Was that just?'

Was that just? That simple question devastated Freddy and made her squirm where she sat. Frantic with fear for Ben, motivated only by her fierce need to go to his aid, she had closed her eyes to the injustice of what she was doing to Jaspar al-Husayn. Shame had touched her but she had refused to surrender to that prompting or to pause and consider what her demand might mean to him. Now colliding with scorching dark golden eyes that glittered like flames, she saw the tough masculine pride she had dented.

'You're an intelligent man. You can't tell me you want to sleep with me just to level the score,' Freddy muttered in an awkward rush, tense fingers locked together and flexing and unflexing. 'I mean…that would just be silly and not at all sensible.'

'Sensible…' Jaspar flung back his darkly handsome head and laughed outright, making her flinch. In a lithe movement, he shrugged out of his jacket and tossed it carelessly on the inlaid chest at the foot of the bed. He undid his collar and cast his tie aside as well.

'I don't feel…*sensible*,' Jaspar imparted in his accented drawl, turning that single word into a mocking retaliation.

Freddy tried and failed to swallow. Transfixed where she sat, she stared at him. Her speech about not being silly and being sensible had been an infallible passion killer on all the hopeful men preceding him, but he had shrugged it off without hesitation. Standing there, long brown fingers engaged in slowly unbuttoning his silk shirt, he challenged her with his stunning eyes, all earthy masculinity and raw sex appeal backed by rock-solid confidence. No, not sensible, she thought abstractedly, mesmerised involuntarily by the aura of the untamed that he emanated. He was of a breed of male utterly unknown to her.

'You hardly know me…' Freddy reasoned weakly.

'I know *too* much.' Strolling forward, light as a big cat on his feet, Jaspar made that wry quip and reached down to raise her upright. He eased the jacket from her slight shoulders, let it drop to the floor and feasted his attention on the burgeoning swell of her lush breasts beneath the taut fabric of her camisole. She backed away, almost tripped over the chaise longue in her haste, a tiny pulse flickering like mad in the hollow of her collar-bone and pounding out her tension.

He was poised several feet away, from his wide shoulders to his taut stomach and long, powerful thighs, incredibly male. Her breath was coming in choppy little bursts from her lungs, her heart hammering, for she could feel her own weakness threatening to break like a dam inside her. He only had to look at her and she wanted him with a deep, fierce craving that terrified her. He made her want what she had never wanted, made her feel as she had never felt. For the first time in her life she felt wildly feminine and desirable and that was a shockingly seductive sensation.

'What are you afraid of?' he asked lazily.

She tensed even more, unnerved by his perception, afraid he might see that she was afraid of herself, of the power he had over her, of the lure of sexual hunger and curiosity. But, worst of all, the frightening urge she had to simply surrender to her own darkest urges, disregarding everything she had always held dear. Freddy had always thought she was a very sensible young woman, but somehow she had roved wildly off course the instant Jaspar had come into her life. Over the past couple of days, she had done crazy things, things she had never dreamt she might do, and now there was a very strong part of her just longing to live out the sheer fantasy of being wanted by such a male.

'Nothing.' The silence seemed to eddy around her like a rippling pool.

He tugged his shirt from the waistband of his tailored trousers and it fell open on a bronzed slice of muscular hair-roughened chest.

'It is only sex...' Jaspar mused with magnificent nonchalance.

'Only sex...' Her voice shook a little, mouth dry, throat tight, her entire being achingly aware of him and of the tightly beaded tingling peaks of her breasts.

'Live a little,' Ruth had once urged her in exasperation but Freddy did not think that Jaspar quite fell within that category. Jaspar was in a major category all of his own, labelled wicked temptation, a moral challenge to be denied. *Only sex?* A mental chasm wider than the Arabian Gulf divided them. Who is ever likely to find out? a sneaky little voice whispered inside her head. Maybe she could just enjoy *him* as an experience. After all, they were married, she found herself suddenly thinking, clinging to a technicality that just minutes earlier she would have scorned.

Jaspar stretched out a lean hand, an expectant look in his imperious gaze that just sent every pulse she possessed crazy. Her resistance crumbled as she meshed dizzily with his glorious eyes and later she had not the smallest memory of her feet carrying her over to his side, only of the devastating kiss that engulfed her in an erotic fire of anticipation.

'I like the zip,' he remarked, settling her back from him to score a considering fingertip along the zip that was straining over her breasts. 'Very tantalising. If you'd removed the jacket when we were airborne, I do believe I would have succumbed to the invitation.'

She was naked beneath the top for she had found it impossible to get the zip done up over a bra. 'Too many pizzas...' she mumbled in guilty disarray. 'Or maybe it was the fudge.'

Jaspar's inky, spiky lashes swept up on bemused golden eyes. 'Fudge?'

In her mind's eye, she saw herself hovering there muttering a confessional like a woman who had cheated on a diet and she cringed for herself, but she just could not think straight that close to him. Not with her mouth still swollen from his, her mind in free fall and her knees wobbling under her. He was like fudge, she thought helplessly. She could still *taste* him, warm and sexy and the last word in mind-bending pleasure.

'Fudge…' Jaspar repeated afresh and, laughing huskily, he backed her towards the bed.

As she rested back against the edge he caught her against his lean, hard, muscular frame and slid down the zip on her skirt. In haste she sucked her tummy in and prayed for the skirt to fall and not linger round her hips like a betrayal. She craved the cover of the sheet. She wanted the curtains closed lest he get too close a look at her flaws and change his mind. She had a sudden image of the phenomenally slight brunette he had thrown out of his bedroom and stopped breathing altogether. The skirt shimmied down in merciful obedience, but then she started thinking about the size of her *derrière* and she was onto that bed so fast, casting off her shoes in haste and seated, she was jet-propelled.

'You are *so* skittish,' Jaspar mused, well-defined brows rising.

Already secure beneath the shield of the sheet, Freddy leant back against the pillows, striving to look amused, cool, woman-of-the-worldish. It was only sex, she reminded herself doggedly. She was twenty-four and a certain scientific interest was as natural as her nerves. But ought she really to be considering sharing a bed with a male whose bedding was still warm from the occupation of her extremely recent predecessor?

In dismay at the reality that she had inexplicably contrived to forget that shattering scene, Freddy asked jerkily. 'Who was that woman?'

Silence stretched.

'Nobody who need concern you,' Jaspar drawled smoothly, but faint dark colour scored his fabulous cheekbones, his expressive mouth hardening. 'She is not and has never been my lover.'

Deeply relieved by that assurance, Freddy could not help thinking that desperation drove Quamari women to serious outer limits in their pursuit of a man. She had been very much shocked by what she had seen, would have been shaken in any circumstances, but had been all the more so at such a scene occurring in a conservative country such as he had sworn Quamar to be. And what might have happened, she wondered grudgingly, had he entered his bedroom alone as the brunette had so evidently expected him to do? Maybe he would have been a pushover for her considerable but slender attractions.

Jaspar shed his shirt in a graceful movement. Freddy was mesmerised by the lean, flexing ripple of his muscles as he moved, the powerful pectorals defined by a triangle of dark, curling hair, his hard, flat stomach. He was like a film unfolding fascinating scene by scene for her. Until she had seen him, she had not believed that a man could be beautiful, but she could not tear her attention from him.

'Do you often get into bed with your clothes on?' Jaspar enquired teasingly.

Rudely reclaimed from her dreaming appraisal, Freddy reddened to the roots of her hair and shrugged and rearranged the sheet. 'It's a little cold up here,' she said in a small voice.

'I'll switch off the air-conditioning.'

Now she was going to roast alive for her foolishness. Below the sheet she began to shimmy by covert degrees out of her tights and shame at her own wanton eagerness engulfed her then. How could she do this? Just give way to lust? That was what it was. She was behaving like a tramp and she was not one whit better than the houri who had greeted him naked on his bed. Beneath the concealment of her lashes, she stole a glance back at him, her nervous tension rising as she noticed, really could not avoid noticing, the definitive cling of his boxer shorts to the aggressive bulge of his masculine arousal.

'Your ears have turned bright red,' Jaspar commented.

Freddy raised frantic hands and buried the offending parts below her tumbling curls, cringing at the recollection of the teasing she had once suffered at school for that same telling symptom of embarrassment. 'Really?'

Shedding his boxer shorts without an audience at that point, Jaspar added to his crimes by throwing back the sheet, but as at that same moment he laced one sure hand into her hair and brought his hot mouth down with devouring hunger onto hers she failed to notice.

'I am so hot for you, *ma belle*,' he husked, his breath fanning her cheekbone.

He was calling her beautiful in French. Wholly entranced, Freddy sunk back into her dream state, laced two daring hands into his thick black hair and looked up at him with rapt eyes of dazed appreciation. 'Kiss me again.'

He kissed her breathless. She was drowning in the hot musky male scent of him, exulting in the seductive weight of him as he rested against her thigh. He undid the camisole zip inch by inch until she was in an agony of fevered anticipation. He slid a hand beneath the parted edges and even before he made contact with her flesh she was on a high, so that when he actually moulded his hand to the full, firm thrust of her swollen breast, the pent-up breath hissed from her parted lips in a long, sighing moan.

'Oh…' Freddy gasped, spine arching as he stroked the sensitised mound and lingered to toy with a distended rosy nipple.

Sweet sensation made her ache. He captured a throbbing tip between his lips, lashed the straining peak with his tongue, teased with his teeth. Within seconds of that tormenting rush of exquisite feeling, Freddy was lost.

'You have delectable breasts,' Jaspar muttered hungrily.

If this was a dream, she didn't want to wake up, Freddy reasoned feverishly. Hot and self-conscious as he scanned her ripe curves with apparent male appreciation, she raised herself from the pillows to let him remove the camisole. And all the time *she* savoured *him*: the silken crescent of his black lashes, the hard slant of his cheekbones, the stubborn thrust of his jawline, the silky feel of his hair below her fingers, the smooth satin skin of his wide shoulders. As his lashes lifted, she drowned in the smouldering heat of his appraisal and never wanted to breathe ordinary oxygenated air again.

'I think you're gorgeous,' Freddy heard herself whisper in reward.

Jaspar gave her a slashing wolfish smile that made her heart jump like a jack-in-the-box. The strangest swell of emotion filled her to overflowing. He probably said that kind of stuff to all his lovers, but he spoke with such sincerity that she just wanted to wrap her arms round him and hug him tight. For the very first time in her life, she was feeling beautiful and sexy and nothing had ever felt so good.

Jaspar readdressed his attention to the creamy swell of her breasts, letting the tip of his tongue trace the tempting valley between while rolling the quivering pink buds, already damp from his ministrations, between expert fingers. And she flung her head back, giving herself up to a kind of enraptured torment she had not even known existed, her breath wrung from her in tortured little gasps.

'You're exquisite,' Jaspar savoured, claiming a passionate and provocative kiss, reacting to the wildness of her response with a hungry, driving urgency that sent her arching mindlessly up to him. 'Blackmail pays unexpected dividends, *ma belle*.'

Blackmail. The word trickled into a mind shut down on an overload of pleasure. 'Jaspar...' she moaned, hauling him back down to her again.

He laughed against her seeking lips, teased her with his tongue, plunging and then withdrawing with erotic mastery, sending the feverish hunger inside her climbing higher and higher until she twisted and squirmed beneath the onslaught. He leant back from her, drew up her knees, slid a hand beneath her hips and skimmed off her panties. She tensed, momentarily dredged back to the real world, suddenly conscious of her own nudity, what she was doing and an incipient flare of panic.

'You match my passion.' Like a sleek predator in vibrant bronze, Jaspar leant over her, fading light gleaming over his tousled hair and illuminating his eyes to a drugging gold intoxication that she was defenceless against. 'I *knew* you would,' he growled with raw satisfaction.

She was melted honey again, going with the flow, lost in the depths of those extraordinary eyes, every inch of her on a high of sensitised awareness so that when he skimmed his fingertips over her stomach to the cluster of pale curls below, her thighs parted on an instinct as old as time. She was achingly conscious of the slick wet heat at the heart of her, the thrumming pulse of almost unbearable tension and craving.

And when he found the tender bud in that secret place, a wave of sensation flooded her in a surge of excitement so powerful, she went out of control. Any sense of time or space vanished. She writhed beneath an exploration that plunged her into sensual abandonment, conscious of nothing but him and the breathless, glorious, agonising pleasure of what he was doing to her frantic body.

'Please...' she whimpered, arching like a cat up to him, unable to stay still, wanting, needing, but totally unable to find the words.

Eyes ablaze with molten hunger, Jaspar slid over her and tipped her up to receive him. She tensed as she felt the hot, hard probe of his shaft against her warm, damp entrance, but white-hot need controlled her, vanquished that flash of fear of the unknown. He drove into her with all the forceful passion she had invited and the sharp stab of pain as he penetrated her tender sheath startled her into a cry.

Jaspar stilled to frown down at her in surprise. 'I'm hurting you?'

'No...' Freddy gasped, eyes tight shut against the threat

of his, in dismay and embarrassment at that unexpected hurt.

He shifted over her. 'You're very small,' he muttered on a sensual groan of combined pleasure and concern. 'But I burn for you, *ma belle.*'

'Don't stop…' She was all shaken up, but the banked-up excitement was still rippling through her in a desperate driving wave of craving.

He didn't stop. He eased further into her with a lithe but controlled undulation of his lean hips and she was entranced by that new sensation, shamelessly hungry for more. He set up a fluid rhythm that sent her heart rate to a thunder in her own eardrums, the explosive passion seizing her again. She angled up to him, helplessly urging him on, wanting, wanting…*wanting* and then finally, when she could bear the suspense no longer and when every nerve-ending was screaming, he sent her flying to a peak of ecstatic release. Glorious splintering sensation cascaded through her convulsed body. He shuddered over her with a harsh cry of male satisfaction and she closed round him like a cocoon, in the grip of wondering contentment.

Jaspar raised his dark head and studied her with crystal-clear tawny eyes. 'I'm sorry I was so rough. I've never hurt a woman like that before—'

'No…no,' Freddy muttered, raising her fingertips like a gentle silencer to his beautiful mouth. 'It was nothing—'

He pushed straying curls back from her brow in a gesture that squeezed her all too susceptible heart. *'But—'*

'Shush.' Unable to continue meeting his gaze lest he recognise her intense mortification, Freddy kissed the only bit of him within reasonable reach, his stubborn jawline. For a split second he tensed beneath that affectionate salutation, and then he laughed huskily and threw himself back against the pillows in a careless sprawl, carrying her with him.

'Now I can face an audience with my father. Sex is a wonderful release for tension, *ma belle.*' Jaspar informed her indolently, lean fingers idly toying with a long blonde curl. 'We will have a good time together while you are here.'

That fast, Freddy wanted to hit him. *A wonderful release for tension?* How could he so degrade what they had shared? As if he had had a strenuous stress-busting game of squash or something? That lovely addictive sense of intimacy and warmth felt totally destroyed in the wake of such casual, unfeeling dismissal. And, that quickly, she began sinking back into her normal self, only to be almost exploded back out of that no-longer safe shell by a true appreciation of what she had just done. About then she also recalled his comment about blackmail paying unexpected dividends and shame settled like a lump of lead in her tummy and expanded exponentially.

Supremely impervious to such sensitivity, Jaspar shifted her off his sprawled length with easy strength, threw back the sheet on his side and sprang off the bed. He vanished into an adjoining room and within the space of minutes she heard a shower running. She rolled onto her tummy. It was much, much too late to be having second thoughts, she told herself unhappily, but, even so, she was in turmoil. Every confused emotion felt ragged and magnified and tears threatened far too close to the surface. She had feelings for *him* that until that moment she had refused to recognise, but she shrank from examining what those feelings were.

She listened to the sound of drawers and cupboard doors opening and shutting from yet another room. He was getting dressed.

'Freddy...?'

Biting her lip, she turned over and sat up, trying to behave normally but with absolutely no idea of what was normal in such a situation.

Damp black hair brushed back from his brow, freshly shaven and dressed in a light grey pinstriped suit, Jaspar looked almost depressingly spectacular and like a Crown

Prince again. It occurred to her that she very much preferred him undressed, shorn of reserve.

'I will see Ben and at the very least get a report on how he has been managing,' Jaspar imparted, grave dark golden eyes resting on her as though willing her to be strong. 'I will try to bring him back here. More than that I cannot promise.'

Her mouth wobbled and she compressed her lips and nodded in mute acceptance.

As Jaspar began to turn away, he suddenly stilled to glance back at the bed. With a sudden imprecation, he flipped the sheet fully back from her.

'What's wrong?' Freddy began, knees raised to her breasts, the ease of sensual oblivion no longer available to her and discomfited shyness gripping her.

Jaspar lifted shaken eyes from the bloodstain on the sheet where he had lain with her.

Belatedly, Freddy registered the same view and she froze in stricken discomfiture. She tried to reclaim the sheet, but with one opposing pull Jaspar hauled it right off the bed.

'I don't believe this but the evidence is hard to ignore,' Jaspar breathed not quite levelly, his dark accented drawl fracturing round the edges. 'If you were a virgin, you *cannot* be my nephew's mother.'

The awful silence felt like a giant weight pressing down on Freddy.

CHAPTER SIX

SHORN of even the top sheet for cover, Freddy was frozen to the mattress and pale as death.

Jaspar's commanding gaze demanded answers but, foolishly, she just wanted to vanish and never ever be forced to see him again. How stupid she had been not to appreciate that, if she became intimate with him, he might realise that she was not the experienced lover he would naturally have expected. She had not foreseen the start of pain that had first betrayed her when they had made love or the possibility of physical proof of her virginity. After all, hadn't she once read that men could often not tell the difference and that certain sports made an actual barrier less likely?

'Who are you?' Jaspar demanded, so low and raw in tone that she shivered in the ghastly quiet that awaited her explanation.

And Freddy knew that she had no option but to tell the truth for nothing else would suffice, and she could have wept at the humiliation she had brought down on herself. Sitting naked on his bed was not the most conducive of positions from which to confess to a guy who was going to be, quite understandably, *very* angry with her.

'Answer me,' Jaspar urged with lethal force.

Freddy trembled, her damp skin chilling even in the warmth of the room. 'Can I get dressed first?'

'No.'

Freddy's eyes stung and glistened as she stared a hole in the offending sheet.

'Before I lose my temper, start talking,' Jaspar advised.

'Erica...Ben's mother died on the ski slopes in an acci-

dent nearly two months ago,' Freddy whispered brokenly and she twisted her restive fingers together round her knees. 'She was my cousin. We had the same name—'

'The same name? What nonsense is this?' Jaspar cut in with savage impatience.

'Our fathers were brothers so we were both Suttons and we were also both christened Frederica. It's a family name. When I was eight, Erica lost her parents and came to live with us—'

'You are trying to tell me that there were *two* of you?' Jaspar launched at her with ringing incredulity. 'Look at me before I haul you out of that bed and force the truth from you!'

Freddy flinched and looked up, clashing with flaming golden eyes that struck her like a whiplash scoring tender skin. 'I lived with Erica. The apartment and everything was hers…but I've been looking after Ben since the day he was born,' she hastened to tell him, her strained voice shaking. 'I'm Ben's nanny.'

'You're the…*nanny*?' Jaspar stared at her with blistering disbelief. 'You were your cousin's servant?'

Freddy's face flamed and she bowed her head down over knees, slowly tightening and closing up into a smaller and smaller ever-shrinking ball. So that was how he regarded her standing as a nanny. A servant. Well, how else had she imagined he might look on her? From the vantage point of his own very superior status, what else could a nanny be on his terms?

'Yet you made me marry you,' Jaspar continued in thunderous continuance, striding to the foot of the bed to snatch up the sheet and toss it in a contemptuous heap at her curling toes. 'Don't try to make me feel sorry for you. I'm not impressed for you didn't shrink from lying deceit and blackmail. If I threw you naked from my home in disgust, who would blame me?'

Her head shot up, panic stamped in her ashen face.

'But if you're telling me the truth and you did share your cousin's name, you are still my wife. Yet you are an impostor and a cheat for you are *not* Ben's mother and can have had no rights over him!' Jaspar decreed in dark fury. 'But I will deal with you later. At this moment, my father awaits me.'

Jaspar strode out to the landing and fought a powerful desire to go back and wrench a fuller confession from her. Though at least she had not belonged to Adil first and indeed was unlikely ever to have met his late brother. Yet that was irrelevant, Jaspar decided, furious that that single point in her favour should have even entered his mind. The real Erica Sutton had had many flaws, but the one sin that could not be laid at the door of Ben's true mother had been that of pretending to be anything other than she was. Relying on that investigative report, he had allowed himself to be trapped into marriage by a scheming, opportunistic liar. The 'devoted' nanny. Sabirah and then *this* in the same day. Fierce anger hardened in him.

As the sun went down an hour later, Freddy stood in the air-conditioned cool of a spacious reception room on the ground floor and watched the cascade of peach, scarlet and gold radiating in a glorious starburst across the horizon. Showered and clad in a light summer dress that had no pretension towards fashion, she was thinking that she had only herself to blame for her present predicament. Jaspar would not even consider reuniting her with Ben now. She was Ben's nanny, not his mother and, what was more, Jaspar was absolutely disgusted with her. She had seen the cold distance slot into his dark eyes like a door slamming shut in her shaken face.

Well, what more had she expected from him? In pursuit of what she had seen as being in Ben's benefit, she had played a rotten devious trick on Jaspar. It was bad enough that she had given him no choice other than to marry her. But for him to discover that she was not even the woman he had believed she was, and that she had had no right whatsoever to have made such a demand on Ben's behalf, had to have been the absolute last straw. Never had Freddy hit a lower ebb or fought harder to hold back tears, for she did not feel right then that she deserved to wallow in self-pity.

She was so ashamed of herself. So much grief and regret but all to what purpose? Why hadn't she appreciated that when the truth came out she would make an enemy of the one individual in Quamar who might have helped her? But then she had refused even to think about *when* she might finally have told the truth. For she had known that her only strength had lain in her masquerade and that, bereft of that pretence, she was powerless to engage Jaspar's compassion. And, that very evening, she had seen his sympathy over her enforced separation from the child that she loved. But she would not see that again, would she?

How could she have gone to bed with him? The dulled intimate ache at the heart of her body was a mortifying reminder of that ultimate and least forgivable mistake. Even knowing that she had to get a grip on her response to Jaspar al-Husayn, at the first challenge she had given way to temptation. Given way so fast too that she burned all over just thinking about how *easily* she had talked herself out of her own principles. Being used as a release for tension seemed a just reward for such cheap behaviour. Furthermore, engaging in that intimacy while still pretending to be Ben's mother could only have worsened her offence in his eyes and would act as another nail in her lying, deceitful coffin.

At eight the following morning, Jaspar emerged from the helicopter with his nephew clinging to him like a limpet.

'Feddy?' Ben prompted anxiously for about the hundredth time since he had wakened earlier, 'Ben want Feddy.'

'Freddy...' Jaspar corrected for at least the fiftieth time. 'She's here.'

The royal nursery staff had conducted an exhaustive enquiry into what a 'Feddy' might be, so that it might be supplied to soothe Ben, but had naturally drawn a blank in their attempt to identify what they had assumed was a much-loved toy. Of course, had his nephew asked repeatedly for his mother, there would have been no such misunderstanding, but no such word had emerged from the little boy since his arrival.

'Feddy...' Ben's bottom lip trembled, huge brown eyes misting with disappointed tears, his lack of trust that the person he wanted would appear patent.

His strong face clenching at the recollection of his nephew's innocent, trusting confidence barely forty-eight hours earlier in London and the obvious damage that had resulted from his sudden loss of all that was familiar to him, Jaspar's arms tightened round his brother's child. That same day in London, he had known the minute that Ben had smiled at him that, without a shadow of a doubt, the child was an al-Husayn for when Ben smiled, it was Adil's smile.

Freddy had not heard the helicopter for the walls of the Anhara palace were thick. Having fallen asleep on a sofa in the early hours while she'd sat up awaiting Jaspar's return and news of Ben, all she had had from the breakfast tray brought to her was a cup of tea. As she paced the beautiful mosaic-tiled floor, she was wondering fearfully why Jaspar had been away for the whole night. Was he even *coming* back?

Pale and drawn, she glanced towards the door when she heard steps echoing in the vast hallway beyond. And then Jaspar appeared on the threshold. His lean, powerful face taut, his hard dark eyes struck hers in a look as physically arresting as a blow. Only as she evaded that grave appraisal that judged and found her wanting did she have the space to notice the little boy he was lowering to the floor.

Her throat burned and she couldn't breathe. For a split second she was paralysed to the spot for she had been fully convinced that, after what Jaspar had discovered about her, he would make no effort at all to reunite her with Ben.

'Feddy…?' Ben whimpered on the back of a doubting sob.

And Freddy just ran, covered twenty feet in seconds to come down on her knees and scoop Ben up into her arms and hold him tight. She could hardly keep her voice under control as she muttered inarticulate things in her eagerness to comfort him. His tiny fingers gripped her tight, his sturdy little body trembling against her. She kissed and hugged him over and over again, held him back from her with overflowing eyes just to look at him, even managing to bring a watery smile to her lips for his benefit. As he squirmed back into closer contact, she looked over the top of his curly head, her face wet with tears of relief.

'I'll never be able to thank you enough…I'm really grateful. I know I don't deserve this but, for *his* sake, thank you from the bottom of my heart,' Freddy told Jaspar shakily.

'I don't want your gratitude,' Jaspar breathed, his grim dark-as-night gaze stinging hot pink into her cheeks. 'My nephew is here only because he needs you.'

Freddy dropped her blonde head. 'I accept that.'

'Don't play the martyr,' Jaspar derided. 'You never had the smallest intention of giving him up.'

At that accusation, her head flew up again, aquamarine eyes bright with disagreement. 'I *did*—'

'No, I will not accept that,' Jaspar cut in with ruthless bite. 'You put your own priorities ahead of his needs.'

Stabbed to the heart by that charge, Freddy said painfully, 'That's not how it was.'

'You were his nanny, not his guardian. In comparison with his father's family, what did you have to offer? Security? You were a young, single woman without the independent means necessary even to support him,' Jaspar pointed out with scorn.

'I know but—' She loved Ben so much, she wanted to plead, a sob catching in her convulsed throat.

'He is only two years old but he belongs to a dynasty that has six hundred years of proud heritage to share with him,' Jaspar delivered. 'He needs and deserves far more than you could *ever* have hoped to give him. His birthright is here in Quamar. He will never live in England again.'

'I just love him,' Freddy muttered chokily, struggling to keep her voice level as Ben looked up at her, but she was chilled by that assurance that Erica's son would never return to England.

'Yet when you could have told me that you were his nanny, you chose instead to *lie*—'

'I never actually—'

'A lie of omission is no less a lie,' Jaspar interrupted, one step ahead of her to squash that potential excuse. 'Had you admitted your real identity, I would have brought you to Quamar to ease his path.'

Her strained face tightened. 'I think you'd have been far too angry with me to even consider doing that.'

'Emotion never gets in the way of my intelligence. Nor, it seems, in the way of yours.' His brilliant dark golden eyes were filled with contempt. 'You used my nephew just as much as his neglectful mother did. You saw the chance to advance yourself through him and you grabbed it.'

Cut to the bone by that condemnation, Freddy gasped. 'That's not true!'

Jaspar elevated an ebony brow, his challenging gaze hard

as granite. 'Then why else did you blackmail me into marrying you? And why else were you so willing for that marriage to be consummated?'

Arms cradling Ben, who was demonstrating a contented desire to drift off to sleep, Freddy stared back at Jaspar, painful colour climbing in her cheeks and then draining slowly away again.

'Don't tell me you spread yourself on my bed for greater love of Ben as well,' Jaspar drawled with cutting clarity, eloquent mouth slanting with derision. 'The ultimate sacrifice? Surely not? No, I think you had far less presentable and more ambitious motives for allowing me access to that glorious body of yours. And not one of those motives related to my nephew's welfare.'

Only the knowledge that if she spoke up in her own defence she would inevitably provoke an argument that would disturb and upset Ben kept Freddy silent. But there was now a mutinous curve to her soft mouth and an angry light in her aquamarine eyes. He was twisting events. Who had carried her into that bedroom? Who had been the last word in seductive persuasion? Who had been ruthlessly set on taking advantage of that ceremony at the consulate and consummating their marriage? Who had reminded her that she was his wife, thereby lessening her resistance at the worst possible moment? Him, him, him and *him* again!

'I'm not fighting with you in front of Ben,' Freddy stated tightly.

His strong jawline clenched. 'I don't fight with women.'

But she had no doubt that, should the opportunity arise, he would be a fast learner. Without another word, Jaspar swung round and strode away and, gradually, Freddy started to breathe again.

There had been so much she had wanted to ask him. Was Ben only visiting for a few hours? When did he have to go back to wherever he had come from? Was she likely to see him again? Or was this a single meeting during which she was expected to say goodbye? Sobered by that fear, Freddy no longer felt like arguing about anything. She was lucky she was seeing Ben at all, she conceded wretchedly. Jaspar had said that he had only brought Ben to her because he needed her, which meant that Ben had been unhappy. Her heart sank at that knowledge.

She spent what remained of the morning reuniting Ben with his favourite toys and pursuits. Ben was very clingy and quiet. She caused a stir in the household by personally cooking lunch for him in the vast basement kitchen, which seemed to her next door to medieval although every inch of it was scrupulously clean. After Ben had eaten, she sat with him until he had fallen asleep in the bedroom where she had had their luggage placed. While there, she reflected uneasily on Jaspar's accusations.

He had not yet given her the chance to explain herself, but he was utterly convinced that greed had influenced all her dealings with him. And could she really blame him for his conviction that she was a gold-digging adventuress willing to use even sex as a means of placation? After all, Erica had been free with her favours and very fond of money. Indeed, her cousin had been downright mercenary with her lovers, even boasting about how generous a settlement she had won in return for her silence about her son's parentage, and Jaspar could well be aware of that fact. So, when Freddy had concealed her identity and had then demanded that he marry her, well, he wasn't likely to think of her as a pleasant, trustworthy or morally upright person, was he?

About twenty minutes later, leaving one of the maids to sit with Ben, she went off in reluctant search of Jaspar. She caught a glimpse of herself in a tall mirror and stopped to stare. Her hair was a riot of curls, her face was bare of make-up and her print dress was pretty shapeless. She found herself wanting to go and do herself up and she shook her head in bewildered impatience at the vagaries of her own mind. *He* wouldn't care what she looked like and she had no business caring. Since when had she been worried about her appearance? Only since a dark accented drawl had murmured, *'ma belle,'* she acknowledged, ashamed of her own weakness.

Finally having to ask for assistance from the manservant who seemed to be in charge of the staff and who spoke excellent English, Freddy was led to a door and abandoned there. She knocked, waited and, not receiving an answer, she went in.

Jaspar swung round from the window where he had been poised, a questioning look of anger burnishing his eyes, accentuating the set of his fabulous bone structure. It was obvious that he had had no intention of answering that knock on the door.

'I'm sorry…I thought it was OK just to come in,' Freddy said awkwardly.

Since his return, Jaspar had changed into a casual white shirt and beautifully tailored beige chinos. She was trying very hard not to look at him direct, but, from the instant she saw him without Ben's presence as a distraction, it was as if he were a giant magnet and she could not resist the pull. His breathtaking dark good looks made the breath catch in her throat. From the hard, angular set of his features to the leashed, muscular power of his lean, well-built frame, he was overwhelmingly male.

Assailed by a compulsive tide of memories from the day before, Freddy was plunged into an agony of tongue-tied discomfiture. One after another those images came at her: the lean, tensile strength of him against her, the excitement of his mouth and his hands on her, the wild, terrifying intensity of her own pleasure. Feverishly flushed, she felt her body quicken and heat in direct response to what was in her own mind and perspiration filmed her short upper lip as she tore her attention from him, appalled that she could have so little control over herself.

'I came here to talk to you,' Freddy mumbled in a stifled voice. 'But now that I'm on the spot, I don't know where to start.'

'What have we left to discuss?' Jaspar murmured low and deep, setting up a chain reaction down her taut spine with the dark, evocative timbre of his drawl. 'Ben? He stays here with us. Eventually he will visit my father several times a week but not until he has settled down again.'

Wondering how on earth he could have managed to extract such a far-reaching agreement from the ruthless older man, Freddy muttered in confusion, 'That sounds great but...well, how is that kind of arrangement going to be possible?'

'For Ben's sake, it *has* to be possible. He is unhappy in my father's household and you cannot be with him there because you are my wife.'

'You could just let me say that I'm his English nanny,' Freddy pointed out in a tentative tone. 'Then... er...perhaps, I could go back there with him.'

'It's too late for that now. My father is aware of our marriage and also that Ben's mother is dead. Naturally, he is displeased that you have become my wife, but, had you been your cousin he would have been outraged.'

Listening to him, Freddy's lips parted and she said in horror. 'You told him...*everything*?'

Jaspar dealt her a grim smile. 'What I tell my father is no concern of yours.'

In receipt of that unapologetic snub, Freddy reddened, but since she hoped he had massaged the truth more than a little it was not a subject on which she was inclined to linger. 'I never dreamt this would all get so complicated—'

'You're not that naive. You didn't care.' His strong jaw-line taut, Jaspar spoke with harsh clarity. 'I'm not ashamed to admit that I did not feel the need to personally shoulder responsibility for my brother's child yet you have forced me to do so. Had I not insisted that your presence was necessary to Ben and that *I* would raise him, I could not have brought him back here today.'

By the time that Jaspar had completed that revealing speech, Freddy was in shock and very pale. She was appalled. She did not know what to say for she had not thought of that kind of consequence, indeed had never really thought beyond her longing to hold Ben in her arms again or her determination to ensure that he had a secure future.

'Ben was miserable without you and, although he would eventually have forgotten you, I could not stand by and watch him suffer. He is Adil's son and I *loved* my brother,' Jaspar breathed in a driven undertone, dark golden eyes glittering a warning as though he was waiting for her to make some comment likely to offend. 'Adil would have taken my child without thought and brought him up. He had a huge heart. I'm afraid I'm not quite so big in the heart department.'

'I didn't mean to do *anything* that would make you feel that you had to bring up Ben yourself.' The most awful feeling of guilt was closing in on Freddy for she both understood his feelings and respected his honesty. There was no reason why he should have felt otherwise. By all accounts, Adil had been a hopeless womaniser and it was hardly fair that Jaspar should find himself having to deal with the consequences. After all, Ben's own father had made no such sacrifices on his child's behalf and Jaspar was a young, single male—well, he would be single again soon, she reminded herself uneasily.

Jaspar vented a humourless laugh. 'I planted the very seed that prompted you to demand that I marry you.'

She blinked. 'What are you talking about?'

'I told you that if I *had* been married, Ben might've been passed off as a relative from my wife's side of the family, thereby enabling me and my then non-existent wife to give him a home,' Jaspar reminded her with dark derision. 'Don't tell me that it's a miracle that we are now in that exact position.'

'That wasn't what gave me the idea,' Freddy protested tautly. 'In London, I felt powerless…and after Ben vanished, how could I trust that you or your family had decent and caring intentions towards him? Right-thinking people don't behave like that. When your father had him snatched, I thought he had to be an absolute monster—'

'He doesn't regard removing Ben from London in that light. He believed that he was rescuing his grandson from neglect, and had you admitted that Ben's mother was dead my nephew would not have been taken. Secure in the knowledge that we were Ben's closest relatives and that he was safe from harm in your care, my father would have been content to wait a few days longer.'

Her face fell, her troubled eyes dropping from the cold condemnation in his for she had explained herself to the best of her ability but failed to make the smallest impression on him. 'I'm sorry…but I don't think I really follow what's happening now,' she confided truthfully, the band of tightening tension round her temples threatening the onset of a headache. 'When do we get a divorce?'

'We *don't*…at least not in the foreseeable future,' Jaspar delivered with a stark bitterness that he made no attempt to hide. 'I must keep you as my wife.'

Freddy frowned. 'I don't understand.'

'My father could have set our marriage aside because I married you without his consent,' Jaspar admitted grittily. 'But if he did so, you would have to return to England. Ben would then be deprived of you again. As at this moment in time that would break the child's heart, I had no choice but to argue that I wanted our marriage to stand.'

'Oh…' Freddy was bereft of any words of consolation as she finally appreciated the ironic and galling position in which Jaspar had found himself placed. Yet even feeling as he did about her, he had put Ben's happiness first and that made her eyes prickle with tears. She felt so horribly guilty because it really was all her fault.

'My father is now talking in terms of making a public announcement about our marriage,' Jaspar stated flatly.

'You mean…your father's w-willing to accept me?' Freddy stammered in a wobbly voice of disbelief.

'He was and is very keen to see me married and produce an heir.' His expressive mouth compressed to a hard line. 'I said you were pure. That was all he needed to hear—'

Freddy gave him an aghast look. 'You let your father know I was a virgin?'

'You have nothing else in your favour,' Jaspar informed her drily. 'Although I suppose you will be wonderfully photogenic.'

'Well, don't you bother agreeing to any public announcements,' Freddy urged him angrily, her temper finally sparking. 'And stop blaming me for everything that's gone wrong! If Ben hadn't been kidnapped, none of this would have happened!'

'But now that it has, recriminations are pointless and, if I have no choice other than to remain married to you, I intend to make use of the situation.' Jaspar sent her a winging glance that had sufficient cool challenge within it to make her tense even more.

Freddy folded her arms, her chin coming up. 'How?'

'You are going to give me a son.'

'Sorry…?' Freddy said with a look of uncertainty, thinking that obviously he could not mean that as it had sounded.

'And I warn you,' Jaspar murmured lazily, his dark drawl

tasting each word with silken precision, 'my brother's wives had a whole string of daughters, so it could take quite some time for us to strike lucky.'

Freddy turned hot pink, opened her mouth, closed it again and then snatched in a ragged breath. 'OK...you've had your joke. Ha ha and all that, but I'm really not in the mood to laugh.'

'That's good, because I'm not joking. You wanted to be my wife and you *are* my wife. Producing heirs to the throne goes with royal territory.' Silent on his feet as a prowling tiger, Jaspar strolled across the distance that separated them and rested reflective dark golden eyes on her bemused face. 'You can bet that I will be home every night this week.'

Freddy retreated a step. 'That's not funny, Jaspar.'

'It wasn't meant to be. My once excellent sense of humour *died* last night while my father was pontificating on whether or not we ought to have a church blessing to mark our union,' Jaspar admitted flatly.

'Oh...my goodness,' Freddy mumbled in the stretched-tight and screaming silence, registering that that discussion had been the ultimate last straw on his terms. 'But surely we can get out of this mess some way—'

'Not while we have Ben to consider—'

'But that doesn't mean it has to be a *real* marriage—'

Jaspar tracked her over to the wall to which she had backed. 'I won't settle for anything less, *ma belle.*'

'But you've been acting like you hate me!' Freddy slung in desperation, her taut shoulder blades finally making contact with the wall.

'Did that stop me taking you to bed yesterday?' Jaspar enquired.

Her cheeks burned. 'No, but—'

'Did you enjoy yourself?' Jaspar incised in a velvet purr.

Her hands knotted into fists by her side and she could no longer look him in the eye. 'That's not the point—'

'It's exactly the point. For a woman who went to shameless lengths to capture me, you're acting very oddly—'

'It wasn't you I wanted to capture…it was Ben!' Freddy snapped between gritted teeth of chagrin. '*Ben* from start to finish—'

Jaspar curved his hands to her waist, drawing her away from the wall.

Her breath tripped in her throat. The sizzle of awareness was in the atmosphere, tensing her muscles, rousing a tiny twisting sensation low in her pelvis. 'Don't you dare,' she warned him nonetheless.

'I always dare,' Jaspar mused, lion gold eyes resting on her soft full mouth until she literally felt them tingle. 'In fact a dare is a challenge—'

'Well, in this case it wasn't.' Freddy backtracked fast, deciding that, with her level of resistance, caution was wiser than foolish valour.

'Tell me you don't want me—'

'I don't want you—'

'And I'll call you a liar.' Jaspar let his hands slide down to the feminine fullness of her hips, easing her inexorably into contact with his hard, muscular frame.

She was trembling, mouth dry, heart hammering. The scent of him was in her nostrils. Warm male overlaid with a faint trace of some aromatic lotion and an extra dimension of something that was uniquely him, something that made her just want to drink him in like an addictive drug, she discovered in dismay.

'Please let go of me…'

Jaspar raised a hand and let his long fingers slowly lace into the fall of her blonde hair. The whole time he kept his striking dark golden eyes nailed to hers. He lowered his dark head, angled her mouth under his and she closed her eyes and swore to herself that she would stand there like an ice sculpture.

A roughened sound of amusement escaping low in his throat, he let the tip of his tongue tease her lips and she jerked, feeling the peaks of her breasts tighten and throb, the sudden surge of heat inside her. As his tongue darted deeper into the tender interior of her mouth, excitement flared like a betrayal inside her and mind over matter was no longer sufficient to restrain her. A stifled moan of frustration was torn from her.

'I desire you,' Jaspar muttered thickly, long fingers gathering up the skirt of her dress, caressing the curve of her hipbone, the shapely length of her thigh as with his other hand he tugged her head back and claimed a devouring kiss that made her dizzy with longing.

She did not want him to stop. She was quivering, pushing herself against him, the damp, hot pulse at the heart of her spurring her on. Hands dropping to below her hips, he lifted her off her feet, crushed her to him, let her feel the unmistakable thrust of his erection, tipped her head back with the passionate urgency of his plundering mouth.

'I want to be inside you, *ma belle*,' Jaspar groaned and on some level she knew that he was bringing her down on a cool, hard surface but she was beyond all thought of intervention.

Sliding her thighs apart, he hauled her back into connection with him. She was burning up, loosing little whimpering sounds low in her throat. With every plunge of his tongue, she wanted more and her skin felt tight and hot, her breasts were aching and her fingers were digging into his luxuriant black hair. And then a sound from the outside world she had forgotten penetrated: the loud, urgent ring of a phone. Her eyes opened and suddenly she was questioning what she was doing and, in instant rejection, pushing herself back from him.

Drawing back, Jaspar breathed unsteadily. 'For once, you are right. This is not the place for this.'

In stricken silence, she stared at him, noting the line of feverish colour accentuating his hard cheekbones, the smouldering blaze of his eyes, and then the frown slowly darkening his lean, bronzed features as though he too was taken aback. Her heart was still pounding as though she had run a three-minute mile. Lowering her head, throat suddenly thick with tears, she slid off his desk and brushed down the skirt of her dress with trembling hands. What had got into her? How could she just lose herself in him the minute he touched her? It was as if a wild, wanton stranger had taken her body over. The force of her own passion shocked her.

Jaspar was speaking on the phone. She would have fled had he not been lounging back against the door. As her attention lingered on him in the most covert of appraisals, she noticed that he was still visibly aroused and her face burned hot. Looking away, she lifted an unsteady hand to her swollen mouth.

Jaspar slung the phone aside again, lean, strong face taut. 'It seems I have a business meeting to attend in New York. My deputy has come down with appendicitis and I'll have to leave immediately. I'll be away for several days.'

'Perhaps you could think over your plans for us while you're away' Freddy muttered unevenly.

Jaspar sent her a penetrating glance and his lean face hardened. 'Was it so conceited of me to imagine that your primary objective was to become my wife and *share* my life?'

Surprised by that question though she was, Freddy was quick to say. 'Yes.'

'Naturally all you were looking forward to was becoming a very wealthy divorcee and duplicating your cousin's success without having to go to the trouble of producing a child,' Jaspar continued with raw derision.

'I've been doing no such thing!' Freddy was disconcerted by the fresh slant his cynical suspicions had taken.

His dark golden eyes arrowed over her unimpressed, his beautiful mouth curling. 'No wonder you're complaining. Instead of shopping until you drop all over Europe and partying, you're going to be my wife—'

'Just how could I have planned to carry on like that when I have Ben to look after?'

'I imagine you'd have hired a nanny as Ben's mother did. You were all set to follow in the family footsteps and why not? What else have you known and what other example would you follow?' Jaspar demanded. 'Your mother deserted you and your father for a richer man and your cousin was equally mercenary in her choice of lovers!'

Freddy looked back at him, aghast at that offensive allegation about her mother coming at her out of nowhere. What on earth was he trying to suggest? What he had just said had no basis in fact whatsoever.

'How dare you insult my mother's memory like that?' Freddy condemned with stricken force. 'My mother did *not* desert my father. She died of pneumonia when I was only two years old!'

Recognising her genuine distress, Jaspar had stilled. His eyes veiled. 'I'm sorry. I should not have descended to that level. That report must have confused your background with your cousin's—'

'No. If you ask me, the idiot that wrote that stupid investigation report just sat in his office and *dreamt* all the dirt of the day up sooner than go and make proper enquiries!' Freddy hurled, far from mollified by that apology. 'Erica's parents were killed in a car crash and were as happily married as my own were. In fact my aunt and uncle were so devoted to each other that they had no time at all to spare for their own daughter.'

'That is as may be—'

'I have very little recollection of my mother.' Freddy breathed painfully, a sob catching in her throat. 'But what I do remember, I *cherish*. Don't you ever dare to say such a thing about her again.'

In a sudden but entirely natural movement, Jaspar reached for her hand as though he would have comforted her, but Freddy snatched her fingers angrily free of his again.

'Do you know what's wrong with you?' she asked fiercely.

Jaspar veiled his eyes. 'I feel sure you're about to tell me.'

'Your life's been too easy and you're judgemental, selfish and insensitive!' Freddy threw at him as she dragged open the door. 'You'll be a lousy king! People make mistakes but sometimes they make them for good reasons as I did and I'm not one bit sorry I'm going to be here for Ben…because you have about as much heart as a stone! And you practically told me that *yourself*!'

And with that final unarguable word on the subject, Freddy stalked out, leaving Jaspar with a very strong urge to smash something.

'You will find great happiness in marriage,' Jaspar's father had been assuring him with galling good humour by the early hours of the morning. 'I had only spoken to your mother twice in the presence of her parents before our wedding but what a joy it was for us to discover each other as man and wife afterwards.'

His wife was finding joy pretty thin on the ground, Jaspar acknowledged, and for some reason that annoyed the hell out of him.

CHAPTER SEVEN

THREE days later, Freddy received her first visit in her role as Jaspar's wife.

In the midst of sorting out the entire wardrobe of little boy's clothes, which had been sent over from the royal palace that morning, Freddy glanced up to see Basmun, the head of the household staff, hovering.

'Yes?' Freddy prompted, reflecting that as news of the fact that she was *married* to Jaspar had spread through the Anhara palace the staff had demonstrated a very different attitude towards her. They no longer avoided looking at her and indeed awarded her an embarrassing degree of respectful attention. She suspected that when she had first arrived they had believed that she was Jaspar's mistress and had been extremely uncomfortable and unsure of how to behave around her.

'Princess Hasna has called, my lady. Refreshments are being prepared,' Basmun said with a low bow.

And who on earth *is* Princess Hasna? Freddy wondered in lively dismay as she tidied her hair and scrutinised her blue cotton skirt and top, deciding that they would have to do for to keep an important guest waiting would be unwise. Presumably the princess was a member of Jaspar's family.

Descending the superb stone staircase, Freddy passed by a gigantic arrangement of pale yellow roses on the lower landing. The beautiful bouquet had arrived for her only the day before. Why Jaspar should have sent her flowers she had no idea, any more than she had yet managed to work out why he had so far phoned her on four separate occasions. He would ask about Ben, enquire about what she was doing, run through his entire daily schedule with her and then assure her that he was looking forward to coming home. Had she not had experience of it four times over, she would have sworn that someone must have had a gun to his head to make him talk in such a civil way to her. If only he had employed some of that time telling her a few facts about his family...

Family, a subject that continually returned to haunt Freddy's own thoughts. Ever since Jaspar had upset her with his mistaken belief that her late mother had deserted her father for another man, Freddy had been feeling uneasy. The allegation niggled at the back of her mind, reminding her of just how little she *did* know about the woman who had brought her into the world. She wanted to see that investigation report for herself and discover how such a crazy misapprehension could have come about. Having made that resolve, Freddy went to meet her important visitor with a lighter heart.

A very attractive girl clad in a fashionable trouser suit rose to greet Freddy with a friendly smile. 'I'm your husband's niece, Hasna, and you are Freddy...or ''Feddy'' as I hear little Ben likes to call you.'

'He still can't get the r sound quite right,' Freddy confided, the worst of her tension evaporating.

'I couldn't wait to meet you.' Hasna's bright blue eyes inspected Freddy with open curiosity. 'But now that I have, I'm not surprised that my uncle Jaspar fell madly in love with you at your first meeting. You're very pretty.'

Somewhat thrown by that speech, Freddy managed to thank her for the compliment but was grateful for the diversion of mint tea and a spectacular array of tiny cakes arriving. Where on earth had Hasna got such a story from? Jaspar madly in love with her? He would cringe if he heard that sort of talk within his own family circle.

'You have certainly put Sabirah's nose out of joint.' Her

visitor grinned. 'She couldn't believe that Jaspar could go off and marry another woman now that she is free.'

'Free?' Freddy prompted, deciding just to plant in the odd encouraging word for it seemed that the youthful Hasna promised to be a mine of information.

'Free to marry again...since my father died.' Hasna's animated face shadowed. 'I miss him very much.'

'I'm sure you do.' And a princess surely had to have a prince for a father. Was Hasna one of Adil's daughters? Freddy paled. Unsettled by Hasna's cheerful reference to Ben and keen to avoid sensitive issues, she murmured hastily, 'You were telling me about this...er...Sabirah.'

Hasna gave her a mischievous smile. 'I think you know very little about our family. Sabirah is my father's widow and only twenty-six years old. He married her five years ago when everybody was expecting Jaspar to marry her.'

'My goodness...' muttered Freddy, no longer so sure she wanted to tap into the mine of information on offer, her tummy giving a nauseous little flip at the concept of Jaspar having *wanted* to marry any woman, for he had definitely not wanted to marry *her*.

'She didn't love my father and, of course, he had no idea that she had been making up to Jaspar too,' Hasna informed her with gathering steam. 'Of course, we hate her. Even though my father passed away only recently, Sabirah immediately began chasing after Jaspar again!'

Still very uncomfortable with the odd feeling of stark hurt that had surfaced a minute earlier, Freddy swallowed back the lump in her throat. She was very much afraid that she had discovered the identity of the naked seductress in Jaspar's bed.

'We were all scared that Jaspar might end up marrying her,' Hasna continued with a grimace. 'Even my grandfather was worried. After all, Jaspar used to be crazy about her and she *is* gorgeous.'

Freddy felt as if someone had put a large foot on top of her lungs for she was finding it hard to breathe. Jaspar had been crazy about Sabirah? Why on earth was she thinking in such an inappropriate way? Hadn't she herself forced Jaspar into what should only have been a marriage on paper? Why was she trying to forget *how* and *why* they had married? Why was she reacting to Hasna's revelations like a normal wife under threat?

'So it's wonderful that you came along and he fell passionately in love with you instead,' Hasna completed with a dreamy expression. 'Some day I want to fall in love like that. How does it feel?'

'Blissful,' Freddy mumbled not quite steadily.

'Can I ask you something?' Hasna leant forward eagerly. 'Is there any truth in the rumour that when Jaspar brought you home on your wedding day, Sabirah was here lying in wait for him?'

'Where on earth did you hear that?' Freddy heard herself ask, her voice sounding to her as though it were coming from the end of a long dark tunnel because she had just had her own worst fears confirmed.

Hasna sighed with patent disappointment. 'You mean...it's not true?'

'Not true.' Freddy preferred to remain sensibly silent on that dangerous subject.

'I suppose that Sabirah getting her comeuppance like that *was* too good to be true,' her visitor conceded with unashamed regret. 'We were all dying to find out.'

'Who's...''we''?' Freddy was keen to leave the entire topic of Sabirah behind.

'Well, there's Medina, my older sister. She's married and her mother was my father's first wife,' Hasna explained. 'After the divorce, he married my mother and she's English just like you and I have two sisters, Taruh and Nura... Sabirah was his third wife.'

Freddy was amazed that Jaspar's late brother had been married three times over but her companion's easy manner with her and her colloquial English were no longer a surprise, particularly when Hasna went on to confide that she and her sisters attended an English boarding-school. An hour later, Hasna's departure left Freddy deep in thought.

Evidently Jaspar's family believed he had succumbed to a whirlwind romance and things that had not made any sense to Freddy were finally falling into place.

Jaspar had been in love with Sabirah before she'd married his brother and presumably Sabirah must have had feelings for Jaspar too. Hasna might well be prejudiced against her stepmother. Perhaps Sabirah had had little choice but to marry Adil: it had to be pretty hard to say no to the heir to the throne when he proposed. But what an appalling situation Jaspar must have found himself in, forced to watch his philandering brother marry the woman that he himself loved. Adil had even fathered Ben while married to Sabirah.

Did that excuse Sabirah for literally throwing herself at Jaspar's head? Could Jaspar have carried on a secret affair with his brother's neglected wife? Freddy doubted that. There was something intrinsically straight and upright about Jaspar. Furthermore, he had been shocked by the sight of Sabirah artistically arranged on his bed and he had gone right ahead and made love to Freddy afterwards, which did not suggest to her much in the way of tortured masculine sensitivity.

However, unless Freddy was very much mistaken, the threat of Sabirah lay behind King Zafir's astonishing acceptance of his son's sudden marriage to a woman he had never even met. She might be a very inferior match for the Crown Prince of Quamar but, as Hasna had confided, her grandfather had been afraid that his son would want to marry his brother's widow and a nobody of an English nanny was obviously considered a lesser evil.

Two days later, Jaspar arrived back earlier than expected.

Without ever admitting the fact to herself, Freddy had spent hours preparing for the event. By seven that evening, her nails were painted blush-pink and her wayward curls had been conditioned into subjection, but she had no make-up on and she had been engaged in trying on every garment that Erica had ever given her. The helicopter came in to land when she was halfway into a short lilac dress with a frilled hem and struggling to get the zip up.

'Oh, no...' she groaned, knowing that she was over-dressed and that she most liked the very first outfit she had previewed. However, cramming her feet into mules, she gathered up Ben, who was already in his pyjamas, and headed for the stairs.

She saw Jaspar first: he was crossing the hall below, lean dark features serious. He looked gorgeous and her heartbeat quickened, her mouth running dry. He tipped his head back and stilled to look up at them. She turned hot pink.

Brilliant dark golden eyes roamed over her and he mounted the stairs to greet them. 'Let me take Ben,' he urged.

Ben went to him without hesitation and started chatting away, excited words tumbling over each other and incomprehensible. Jaspar smiled down at his nephew and the effect of that warm, charismatic smile made her breath catch in her throat.

'He's back to normal already. Just the way I remember him in London, full of life and fearless again,' Jaspar commented with satisfaction.

'Yes...'

'You've worked a real miracle with him.'

'I just play with him and cuddle him...and that's about

it, really,' Freddy muttered, brain as empty as a yawning crater at the moment when she most longed to come off with something if not witty, at least intelligent.

Jaspar strolled down the stairs again and as she drew level with him he turned to study her. 'You look fantastic in that dress,' he murmured with husky appreciation.

'Erica gave it to me but I haven't worn it before...I didn't go to the sort of places where people dress like this,' Freddy muttered in an even more breathless rush, closing her damp palms in on themselves, feeling as if she were on a first date and so awkward her nerves were screaming. So now he was free to wonder why she was parading around in a dress more suited to a flashy nightclub than his home.

'I'll take you shopping. You have no need to wear your cousin's cast-offs now.'

'It's not a cast-off. She bought it for me. She was always very generous and I know you think that she was a hateful person but I cared about her.' Having fired off that heated little speech, Freddy could have bitten her tongue out for right there in front of her his lean, strong face froze.

The silence lay heavy.

'You have a point.' Jaspar took her aback with that sudden agreement. 'If you don't abuse Adil, I'll endeavour to match your generosity where Erica is concerned. Some day we'll have to talk to Ben about his natural parents and we need to take a less emotive view of his past.'

Freddy nodded, the anxious light in her aquamarine eyes clearing. He was talking as though they were likely to be together for a very long time, she was thinking dizzily. But then no other arrangement made sense, did it? Where had her wits been over the past few days? When Jaspar had been talking about her having his children, he would hardly be expecting her to abandon them at some future stage.

His decision to put Ben's needs first and to bring up his

nephew with her meant that their marriage *had* to become a real marriage. Jaspar had had no choice on that score. No more choice than he had had in telling her that she would have to try and give him a son. He needed an heir, whether he liked it or not, whether he wanted to be married to her or not.

Jaspar, she registered, had moved on faster than she had and accepted the inevitable. The beautiful roses and the phone calls had all been part of the same parcel. He was trying to act like a normal husband. Only a normal newly married man might have grabbed his wife after five days away rather than reaching straight for the toddler. Unfortunately, Jaspar was married to a woman whom he would not even have asked out on a date had he ever had the opportunity and practising restraint could hardly be a challenge for him. He had probably hauled her into bed on their wedding night more out of sheer bloody-mindedness than anything else, Freddy decided wretchedly.

Basmun served coffee with great ceremony in the main salon. Jaspar had brought a toy train back from New York for Ben: a motorised engine large enough for Ben to sit on and complete with its own track. Freddy watched Jaspar putting the track together while Basmun strained at the leash to come to his royal employer's assistance, clearly regarding the task as beneath Jaspar's dignity. But Freddy could see for herself that Jaspar was enjoying himself and she was touched by the sight of Ben clumsily attempting to copy his uncle's every move.

'No, not there,' Jaspar told Ben and Ben gave him a hurt look and Jaspar groaned and let the little boy continue to get in his way.

As she watched them together Freddy could see the faint family resemblance between man and boy. When Ben lost the last of his toddler chubbiness he would have much the same nose as his uncle, and the colour of his eyes, if not the set of them, was almost identical. Jaspar would be a great role model for him too.

Her throat tightened. Fate might have put them on opposing sides when they'd first met but she saw so much to admire in Jaspar. His intelligence, his strength, his honesty and family loyalty, not to mention the powerful sense of responsibility that had made him place the needs of a child he barely knew ahead of his own. He didn't lose his cool in a crisis either but had he known the ultimate price that he would pay, she was sure he would never have agreed to marry her.

How could her conscience do anything other than claw at her? She had deprived him of the right to choose his own wife and he was stuck with her. Finally, just at the point where she was beginning to realise that she was falling in love with Jaspar al-Husayn, she was recognising what a humiliating trap she had fashioned for herself. Never would she be able to think that she was wanted for herself or even that he had chosen to be with her. The narrow loveless boundaries of the marriage she had foolishly forced on him would *always* be with them.

Ben fell asleep on top of the toy train. With Freddy leading the way, Jaspar lifted his nephew and carried him upstairs. Having tucked the little boy in for the night, Freddy turned to find Jaspar watching her with a grim light in his gaze.

'I gather you've been sleeping in here as well.' Having thrown a meaningful glance at the less than seductive T-shirt nightwear with its English logo lying on the other single bed in the room, Jaspar strode back out into the corridor.

Freddy was very tense. 'Yes.'

'Didn't you listen to *anything* I said before I left for New York?' Jaspar demanded with considerable impatience.

'You can't share Ben's room like a nursemaid. I've already instructed Basmun to hire a nanny—'

'But that's not necessary—'

'Yes, it is. Ben must learn Arabic as well as English and there will be many occasions when it won't be convenient for you to look after him,' Jaspar retorted levelly. 'Do I really have to spell out to you that a wife shares her husband's bed?'

On the galleried landing, he snapped lean brown fingers in imperious command and issued a clipped instruction to a servant passing through the hall below.

'I shared Ben's room because I thought it would help to make him feel more at home here,' Freddy argued.

'Overkill,' Jaspar pronounced with conviction. 'Did you share his accommodation in London?'

Freddy flushed. 'Occasionally.'

'A maid can sleep in the nursery until a nanny is hired. I'm going for a shower before dinner,' Jaspar completed with icy finality.

'For goodness' sake, after you'd gone, I didn't know *where* I was supposed to sleep!'

Jaspar cast her a gleaming dark golden glance empty of any hint of apology. 'Well, *now* you do.'

Furious with him for making such an issue of the matter, Freddy followed him. 'I'm only just getting used to the idea that we're really married.'

'How strange. That married feeling hit me like a lightning bolt on our wedding day!'

'I don't think you need to be so sarcastic,' Freddy snapped.

'You think not?'

As Freddy entered the bedroom Jaspar swung round, sent the door behind her slamming shut and before she had the slightest idea of his intention he had backed her up against the still-juddering wood. He brought his mouth down with explosive driving heat on hers, strong arms closing round her as he hauled her up to him and melded her slighter length to the hard, muscular power of his own.

He might as well have set off fireworks inside her. She went from angry stiffness to encouraging pliancy, the hunger he unleashed flaming into passionate union with her own. Her head fell back, allowing him to deepen the connection, her lips parting to the erotic penetration of his tongue, a shaken moan dredged from her in response. Sweeping her up into his arms, Jaspar laid her down on the bed and gazed down at her with molten eyes of appreciation for a moment before straightening again.

'Don't worry,' he breathed in a tone of intimate amusement. 'Even a cold shower and a four-course meal couldn't take me off the boil, *ma belle*.'

Mortified by the response he had wrung from her with the barest minimum of effort, Freddy stared up at him while struggling to catch her breath again. 'You can't just expect me to—'

His lean powerful face set taut, brilliant eyes shimmering a warning. 'I expect nothing but a modicum of common sense from you. While the servants believed you were my mistress, they would've vied with each other to be discreet for my benefit, but you're now my acknowledged wife and everything you do is likely to be talked about.'

At that news, Freddy paled. 'Really?'

'What else did you expect when you married a man in my position?' Jaspar demanded in exasperation. 'And if a rumour that our marriage is already so troubled that we occupy separate bedrooms spreads beyond these walls, we have no hope of convincing anybody, least of all my father, that this is the love-match I said it was!'

'Love-match?' Freddy repeated unevenly.

His narrowed gaze darkened, his strong jawline clenching. 'How else do you think I persuaded him to accept our marriage? With the *truth*?'

Pale as milk, Freddy dragged her guilty eyes from him. In that harsh intonation, she recognised his angry regret at the necessity of having had to voice such a lie. She should have had greater faith in what Hasna had said on the same subject.

'It was the only argument I could use,' Jaspar admitted half under his breath, his anger having spent itself. 'His honest pleasure on my behalf shamed me.'

It shamed Freddy too.

'There's really nothing I can say to make things right,' she muttered shakily.

'But I too made mistakes,' Jaspar murmured flatly. 'I didn't want to trawl through the murky secrets of Adil's life and I resented the necessity. I did indeed think of Ben as a parcel who might be tossed on a plane. But, all that is behind us now.'

'How can it be?' Freddy muttered uncomfortably.

'It *has* to be,' Jaspar countered with a level of self-assurance that disconcerted her. 'We have to live together and make a success of our marriage...and why not?'

Disconcerted, Freddy raised her head. A good half-dozen reasons why not were heaped on the tip of her tongue but she remained silent, all too willing to be persuaded otherwise.

'You look surprised.' Jaspar shed his jacket in an indolent, very masculine movement and loosened his tie. 'We'll discuss it over dinner.'

They dined in the formal splendour of a room so large it could have handled a state banquet. Freddy could not help thinking that, with so many other rooms available, a dining-room where their voices did not echo and the servants did not have to trek sixty feet from the door to the table might have been rather more relaxing. Not that Jaspar seemed remotely uncomfortable with his surroundings, however. But then from birth he must have been accustomed to acres of space around him, Freddy thought ruefully, and it was she, rather than Jaspar, who had to adapt to a challenging new environment and a pronounced change in status.

When the coffee was brought, Jaspar lounged back in his carved chair, the very epitome of male relaxation. 'While I was in New York, I looked at our situation from a business point of view...'

'A *business* point of view?' Freddy parroted helplessly.

'Sometimes it's a good idea to examine a problem from a different perspective,' Jaspar informed her. 'I came to the conclusion that marriage has a lot in common with a business deal.'

Barely recovering from the cut inherent in being labelled a problem in his life, Freddy was forced to swallow even more pride in receipt of that concluding statement. 'How can you say that?'

'In the usual scenario, a man and a woman fall in love and marry, each of them armed with an entirely separate set of expectations, and then they either compromise or break up,' Jaspar contended, dark golden eyes lit with supreme cynicism. 'But we're *not* in love and I already know the worst that you are capable of. That has to be an advantage.'

By the time he had finished speaking, Freddy had lost colour. 'Is it?'

'Naturally it is. We have a marriage of convenience, a practical, unemotional arrangement which can satisfy us both in different ways. You will have Ben and the lifestyle that you wanted in return for which—'

'You get...you hope...a son and heir,' Freddy completed doggedly for him, struggling to conceal the tide of angry pain assailing her. After all, if he could sit there discussing their relationship in the most appalling cold-blooded terms, far be it from her to betray any sentimental or sensitive weakness.

'*And* a beautiful and very sexy wife,' Jaspar traded huskily, sensual appreciation lighting his stunning eyes as he surveyed her. 'I see no reason why we shouldn't establish a mutually beneficial relationship. We leave the past behind us and make the most we can of the present.'

Below the level of the table, Freddy's taut fingers were biting into the fine linen napkin on her lap. 'I would need more than that to be happy—'

'You should have thought of that aspect before you married me,' Jaspar countered with lethal cool.

'I didn't know I was going to end up *living* with you, did I?' Freddy snapped, her fragile composure splintering to give vent to the churning emotions she had been fighting to suppress while she listened to him. 'And do you know what I see? Just one more wimpy male who got hurt *once* in his wretched life—'

Jaspar dealt her an incredulous look. 'I beg your pardon?'

'And felt so damned sorry for himself and his wounded pride that he's been taking it out on every woman he's been with since by acting like an absolute four-letter word!' Freddy condemned fiercely, thrusting back her chair to stand up. 'Well, you're not taking it out on me! So if and when you're willing to offer me something other than the *business* blueprint for the marriage from hell, tell me. In the meantime, don't you dare lay a finger on me. I'm out of bounds—'

'You're damned right you are,' Jaspar grated, rising to his full commanding height, a level of scorching anger that shook her blazing in his lean, hard-boned features. 'What is this talk of wimpy males and wounded pride? Where has all this nonsense come from?'

'It's not nonsense,' Freddy told him, her strained voice shaking with the force of her disturbed emotions. 'I wish it was but I honestly believe that you dislike women. I thought it was just me but I don't think it is—'

'Answer the question. To what were you referring? And to whom have you been talking?' Jaspar demanded with charged force.

At that repetition, Freddy paled, for she was already aware that in giving way to her temper she had lost control of her tongue and said far too much, and she certainly did not want to name the source of her information as being a member of his own family. 'I'm sorry if I was offensive...I don't think we should get into that,' she said in a small, tight voice.

'You were referring to Sabirah.' His jawline rock-hard, Jaspar studied her now-reddening face with raw derision.

'What I was trying to say...clumsily,' Freddy conceded in deep discomfiture, 'is that I couldn't face having a baby with someone who talks about us having an *unemotional* arrangement. I do have feelings—'

'Then respect *mine*,' Jaspar breathed in seething condemnation.

As he strode out of the room Freddy braced trembling hands on the table and snatched in a ragged breath. He got much angrier than she did but stayed in control, she thought sickly, running back over her own thoughtless attack on him and the resentment that had prompted it. She winced for herself. There he had been telling her that there was no prospect of him ever developing a warmer attachment to her and, in her hurt and disappointment, she had lashed out at him on a subject she should not have broached. Reminding him about Sabirah had been a downright nasty thing to do and, in doing so, she had got exactly what she deserved, hadn't she? For in his volatile reaction, she had seen much that she would sooner not have seen: a pain and bitterness that still lingered five years on. Sabirah had hurt Jaspar a great deal.

A couple of hours later, long after the sun had gone down in a blaze of glory and she had given up hope of Jaspar reappearing, Freddy went upstairs. And on the bed in what she was striving to regard as *their* bedroom, what did she find? A large pile of exquisitely wrapped gifts with a card on top that was inscribed with her name in Jaspar's bold black scrawl.

Her heart sank as if weights had been anchored to it. The first and smallest parcel contained her favourite perfume, which she always wore. She breathed in deep. The second was an opulent jewel case containing a delicate gold watch studded with diamonds. Swallowing hard, she fingered her stainless steel watch that had a bracelet that was forever working itself loose. The third and largest parcel opened to disclose a glorious antique rosewood vanity case filled with gleaming silver-topped containers and a whole array of fascinating items. She gazed at it in frank disbelief. The fourth gift was a designer handbag, similar in style to the bag she used but infinitely superior. And the fifth was an elaborate gilded coffer filled to the brim with…mouth-watering fudge.

Legs feeling wobbly, registering that she was married to a guy with meteoric grasp on the principles of one-upmanship, Freddy folded down in a heap on the soft thick rug beside the bed and stuffed herself with the fudge. If she had been paranoid she might have thought he had bought her all those presents just to make her feel that she was the most hateful woman alive. But she wasn't paranoid. However, she *was* striving to understand why the male who had talked about marriage being on a par with a business deal should have confounded her every expectation and left her reeling.

Those gifts told her so much about Jaspar, she reflected,

still in a daze at his extravagance while she worked her
way steadily through the fudge. He was incredibly obser-
vant. He must have noticed her fiddling with the faulty
catch on her watch and he had identified her perfume, even
recalled the colour and shape of her handbag yet he had
only seen her with it once that she could recall. However,
she had no idea how he had found out that she adored
Victorian things and collected little bits and pieces like but-
ton hooks. He had been so generous, so thoughtful in
choosing presents that would please her that she was
touched to the heart, but also shamed into considerable discomfiture.

A man who disliked women would not have exercised
that degree of care or consideration. No, she was dealing
with a male who simply distrusted women and not without
good reason. A male who had learned to hide his true nature behind a cold front of reserve and a stinging talent in
the field of put-downs. But still a guy who had sent her
roses, phoned her every day and done a heck of a lot of
shopping on her behalf. She smiled through the tears trickling down her cheeks.

A marriage of convenience? Well, considering that she
had blackmailed him into marrying her and then left him
feeling that he had to *stay* married to her for Ben's sake,
she had no right to talk about wanting more. He had had
to settle for less than what he wanted, so she would have
to as well. She wondered how long it would be before she
heard him call her, *'ma belle'* once more and even if he
would ever use those words around her again...

CHAPTER EIGHT

JASPAR eased the bedroom door closed in his wake and then stilled in surprise.

In the moonlight flooding through the windows he could see that Freddy had fallen asleep on the floor. A ring of fudge wrappers and crumpled tissues surrounded her like a statement and he could see that her nose was pink and her eyelashes still clogged together. An unexpected shard of tenderness stirred in him: she looked so small and forlorn. Gathering her up, he laid her down on the bed and unzipped her dress to ease her free of its crumpled folds.

She was so tactless, so utterly lacking in the more subtle feminine wiles of persuasion, that she fascinated him. From an early age Jaspar had been taught never to speak without thought, never to relax his guard and never ever to lose control of his temper. But until Freddy and her towel had exploded into his once smooth and organised existence, his self-discipline had rarely been challenged. After all, people didn't criticise him or argue with him and women had always been eager to please him.

Only Freddy had dared to make demands. Standing there at the dining table ranting and raving at him quite unaware that an aghast Basmun was striving to hurry backwards out of the room again with a heavy tray. She had a lot to learn. Although his father was already testily demanding to know when he could expect to meet his new daughter-in-law, Jaspar felt that he could not risk the potential conflagration. Freddy was a firebrand and his parent's concept of contemporary womanhood was a good half-century out of date.

Freddy came awake with a sleepy sigh and focused on

Jaspar. Moonlight gleamed over his black hair, mirrored the sheen of his dark eyes, marked the bold angles of his hard cheekbones and shaded the hollows. She sat up with a start. 'Where have you been?'

'Working in my office—'

'I didn't even think of looking there for you. I thought you'd gone out—'

'There's not a lot in the immediate radius of the Anhara.' Stretching out a lean hand, Jaspar switched on the lamps by the bed.

Blinking in the sudden light, registering that he must have removed her dress and that she was only wearing a lacy bra and panties, Freddy coloured in confusion. She studied his darkly handsome face and the faint smile curving his mouth and her heart skipped a beat. She was relieved that he was no longer angry, that her thoughtless words had done no lasting damage. 'I'm sorry about what I said. I don't know what gets into me around you. I don't say nasty things to other people,' she muttered defensively.

'It's forgotten.' Tipping his proud dark head back, Jaspar gazed down at her, eyes a stunning lambent gold beneath dense black lashes. 'In certain moods, I love to provoke.'

As her mouth ran dry her breath feathered in her throat. She was electrified by the look in his eyes, the hungry male appreciation that he made no attempt to hide. 'I have a quick temper.'

'At least you didn't kick me this time,' Jaspar said huskily, reaching behind her with lethal cool to release the catch on her bra.

As he eased the straps down her arms her face flamed, but a hot, tight twist of excitement was unfurling like a dark flower in the pit of her stomach. Her full creamy breasts with their taut rosy peaks spilled from the bra cups, brazenly bare for his appraisal. In the humming silence, she sucked in a quick shallow breath to sustain herself.

'You are magnificent, *ma belle*,' Jaspar rasped in a roughened undertone.

She tingled all over, feeling so aware of him, so suddenly desperate for his touch but, at the same time, wonderfully aware of her own femininity and confident of her power to attract. Obeying a wanton prompting that she could not resist, she found herself tipping back her shoulders and arching her spine so that her shapely curves were all the more prominent.

A driven groan escaped Jaspar and he succumbed to the temptation of that tantalising movement by closing a hand into her hair and dragging her down onto the pillows, following her there with unconcealed impatience to close his mouth with devastating urgency to first one straining nipple and then the other. All the breath in her was drawn out of her in one long keening moan of startled response.

'I am hopelessly in love with your glorious body,' Jaspar confided with ragged fervour.

'Hmm...' Words were beyond her. Her whole being was bound up in the hot provocation of the male fingers kneading her lush breasts and toying with their tender, throbbing peaks. Her hand laced into the silky depths of his thick hair, her hips shifting on the mattress, the thrum of rising heat spreading through her with electrifying intensity. He lashed the rigid tips to tormenting sensitivity with the tip of his tongue and she was gasping for breath, neck arching as she thrust herself helplessly up to him.

'You have a volcanic effect on my libido.' In a lithe movement, Jaspar pulled back from her and sprang off the bed to undress.

'Really?' A dazed sense of achievement assailing her, Freddy watched him rip off his beautifully tailored suit with the kind of impatience that struck her as a considerable compliment. He wanted her. He wanted her something fierce. Never had she dreamt that she could have that kind of effect on a man. Never had she suspected that that knowledge might enable her to lie half naked and unashamed, accepting the burning gold admiration of his eyes on her.

'You are a very sensual woman,' Jaspar told her with husky appreciation.

And he was an incredibly sexy guy, Freddy thought dizzily, losing the lingering remnants of concentration to discover that she could not take her eyes from his lean, well-proportioned physique either. He was all power and potency, all dominant male and muscles from his wide, strong shoulders to his long masculine thighs and so very different from her, for where she was all soft and yielding he was all taut angles and hard, virile promise. 'I don't know what I am,' she confessed. 'I'm only just finding out—'

'Let me show you...' Jaspar breathed, urging her round to face him so that he could slide his hands beneath her hips to skim off the last garment that concealed her from him. 'I've thought of this moment every day I've been away from you, *ma belle*.'

Wholly naked then, she blushed rosily, shy as she had not been seconds earlier, but he came down beside her and claimed her lips with an explicit need that fired her every skincell with passionate response. She reached up to him, holding him to her, glorying in the hair-roughened abrasion of his muscular chest against her tightly beaded nipples, drinking in the familiar male scent of him with heady recognition and rejoicing in the need he made no attempt to hide from her.

He rearranged her on the mattress and plotted an increasingly provocative and tormenting path down over her trembling body. She closed her eyes, head falling back as she gave herself up to the stream of intoxicating sensation, feeling the tightening knot of ever-increasing tension build at the very heart of her where she was hot with helpless longing. And then he eased her thighs apart, found the hottest point of all with his knowing mouth. He sent shellshocked tremors travelling through both her mind and her body and her aquamarine eyes flew wide in dismay.

'No, you can't...' she mumbled.

'Yes, I can,' Jaspar countered thickly. 'I want to drive you out of your mind with pleasure.'

As suggestions went, she considered that one fairly seductive, but inhibition fought with desire until he took decision from her. Just as quickly, what he was doing to her all-too-willing and rebellious body wiped every other consideration from her mind. She hadn't known, indeed could never have dreamt, that she had such a capacity for enjoyment and, having had that fact discovered for her, had no control over the strength of her own response.

'Oh...' She was all liquid heat and burning, her heart hammering so hard that she was panting for breath. A merciless craving for satisfaction was twisting through her writhing length like a tightening red-hot wire.

Just when she was on the quivering brink of that peak, her whole being centred on his every move, Jaspar hauled her under him, tipped her up and sunk into her in one driving thrust. A shocked moan of delight was wrenched from her and then there was only the hot, aching pleasure of his pagan rhythm, the urgent surge of his maleness over and inside her in the mindless union of frantic desire. She rose to meet his every thrust in fevered response until her hunger peaked at an unbearable height and she splintered into what felt like a thousand shining pieces and drowned in the floodtide of exquisite pleasure that followed.

There was something to be said for 'only sex', Freddy conceded in a daze as the tremors of sweet ecstasy only slowly receded from her quivering body. But if he used that phrase again, she would kill him, she *knew* she would.

Yet even as he shuddered over her with an uninhibited groan of fulfilment she was smiling and closing herself round him in a cocoon of loving intimacy. She had blessings to count. He had bought her fudge and he was great with Ben. He loved her body, truly loved her body. He had been made for her; he just didn't know it yet. She let possessive fingers idly thread through the damp, tousled strands of hair at the nape of his neck and skirt round to skim down one angular cheekbone.

Closing his arms round her, Jaspar rolled over so that she lay on top of him. Pushing the tangled blonde curls back from her face with surprising gentleness, he smiled at the feverish flush that merely enhanced the brightness of her aquamarine gaze and traced the reddened curve of her full lower lip with a reflective fingertip. 'Next time you come to New York too, *ma belle.*'

'To help you shop?' Freddy teased.

Reclining back against the banked-up pillows, Jaspar shrugged a broad brown shoulder. 'When I'm in the city, I like to get out for some fresh air between meetings.'

'Oh, I'm not complaining.' Freddy was entranced by the faint defensive air he exuded as if he was just a little self-conscious about having bought so much for her. 'I was just knocked flat by all those pressies and I haven't even said thank you yet.'

'I've had all the thanks I required.' Jaspar gave her a wolfish grin that made her heart tilt on its axis. 'Glad you liked the fudge.'

'I ate the whole box...don't remind me!' Freddy groaned in embarrassment.

Jaspar laughed and shifted her back onto the mattress beside him so that he could gaze down at her discomfited face. His dazzling golden eyes narrowed to a slumbrous level and he lowered his dark head and captured her mouth with a slow, searching sensuality that made her head spin.

A long time later, he carried her into the shower with him. She had not a clue what hour of the night it was by then, but the water cooling her heated skin woke her out of her satiated daze and she remembered the niggling curiosity that had troubled her while he had been abroad. 'That report…that private detective's report that was done on Erica,' she told him. 'I want to see it.'

Jaspar tensed in the loose circle of her arms. 'Why?'

'Nothing in it is likely to shock me,' Freddy pointed out ruefully. 'I did *live* with Erica. But it's really the bit purporting to be about either my mother or hers that I'd like to get a look at.'

'But you said that your mother died when you were a baby. You can hardly doubt such a fact.'

'I *don't* doubt it.' Reluctant to reveal just how uninformative her late father had been on the subject of her mother, Freddy struggled to explain her feelings. 'But naturally I'm curious when something odd like that comes up and it relates to my family.'

Tugging her out of the shower cubicle, Jaspar lifted a big fleecy towel and wrapped her into its folds. 'You should just forget about it. I very much regret having mentioned the matter. In any case, I had the report destroyed.'

'But why?' Freddy gasped.

'I was thinking of Ben. I felt that it would be unwise to retain a document that vilified his mother.'

Seeing his point, Freddy sighed. 'I really did want to see it.'

'But that report was full of errors.' In the midst of towelling his lithe, sun-darkened body dry, Jaspar regarded her in some bewilderment. 'I could have fresh inquiries made by a different agent but I really *don't* see—'

'Yes, I'd like that,' Freddy rushed in to assure him with a vigorous nod of pleased confirmation, her determination to pursue the matter unhidden. 'My pet theory is that my uncle, Erica's father, may have been married before he met her mother and that that first marriage broke up.'

'This long after the event, does it really matter?'

'It does to me.'

'Then it will be done, *ma belle*,' Jaspar asserted levelly.

A warm smile curved her lips. 'How did you know I would like that vanity box?'

Jaspar grimaced and then laughed. 'That report. Your life and your cousin's were blended into one but, once I knew the truth about you, it was easy to work out what related to you rather than to her.'

'Yes. Erica collected miniature alcohol bottles.'

His appreciative golden gaze rested on her twinkling aquamarine eyes and the cheeky smile on her face set between the torrent of wild damp curls tumbling round her shoulders. 'Do you know that the first time I saw you in a towel, I started thinking about mermaids?'

Freddy blinked. 'Mermaids?'

'There's a place in the mountains not too far from here where I used to swim as a boy. Some day I must take you there…' As his roughened drawl dropped in tone to send a responsive shiver down her spine, and she met the smouldering intensity of his stunning eyes, Freddy found herself surging back into his arms at the exact same time as he reached out for her again.

Over four weeks later, Freddy lay on a gorgeous silk woven rug on a grassy bank beneath the spreading shade of a graceful plane tree. It was a glorious spot. Far above a hawk wheeled and dipped against the cloudless blue sky. Rocky hills sheltered the fertile valley floor and spring flowers and vegetation grew all around the lake.

Freddy watched Jaspar dive in a lithe curve into the dappled water, the sunlight turning his wet skin to shimmering bronze. He was so hopelessly energetic, she thought, and she smiled for Jaspar did everything with energy and commitment. Fulfilling his duties as Crown Prince of Quamar might sentence him to listening for hours to the often petty disputes between ordinary Quamaris that were brought to him for settlement in preference to the courts, but he never betrayed any sign of impatience or exasperation.

'I have to be accessible and approachable,' Jaspar had pointed out ruefully only the day before when a particularly complex quarrel over grazing boundaries had been laid before him and had dragged on so long that their afternoon out had had to be cancelled. 'Our people have a great respect for the old ways and so must we.'

Although she was feeling languid and lazy from the heat, she was thirsty and, pushing herself up on one elbow, she dug into the cool-box which was disguised as a giant picnic basket and withdrew a bottle of mineral water and a glass. As she sat up a faint sensation of dizziness made her head swim and she blinked. That was the second time in a matter of days that she had felt woozy and she was conscious that her period was a little overdue. But then in the past her cycle had been disturbed before by foreign travel and even by emotional upsets and there was no denying that her life had changed out of all recognition over the past six weeks. She wondered if it was too soon to do a pregnancy test, but also felt that the chances of her having conceived the very first month of their marriage were slim.

Although Jaspar *did* make love to her just about every day of the week, she conceded, watching him work off his surplus energy in the water, her gaze possessive and tender. She was head over heels in love and the past month had been a revelation to her for she had simply never been so happy. As each sunlit day melted into another beautiful sunset, she felt more secure in that happiness. No matter what other demands were made on him, Jaspar devoted a great deal of time to her and Ben.

Of course, he had said that they would have to make a success of their marriage. But the way he talked to her and sought her out to share little things with her had made Freddy hope that there was rather less hard work involved in making a go of things than those warning words of his had originally made her fear. Jaspar genuinely seemed to *want* to be with her and his affection for Ben was patent. However, when it came to more personal feelings, Jaspar was very much more reserved.

Oh, he told her she was beautiful so often that she was almost beginning to think that she might be, she reflected with helpless amusement. And he laughed when she joked, and in turn he teased her, and they had a wonderful easy camaraderie that was nonetheless equally given to erotic interludes because he was a very passionate guy. So he found her desirable and he enjoyed her company. He was fond of her but he would never love her and she could hardly blame him for that. Love either happened or it didn't and if it hadn't happened yet, it would never happen.

Stark naked and magnificent, Jaspar padded up to lift a towel. 'Some mermaid,' he chided with vibrantly amused eyes. 'Lying here in sloth on the bank.'

'One dip a day is enough for me and, after eating so much, I feel totally lazy,' Freddy confided, mouth running dry at the sight of him, heartbeat quickening in concert.

'You're still tired? But you had a nap—'

'I didn't. I was just lying with my eyes closed—'

'I walked over here and spoke to you. You were *fast* asleep.' Jaspar pulled on khaki chinos.

Her gaze rested on his powerful torso, the whipcord ripple of muscle as his arms flexed. The tantalising little furrow of dark hair that dissected his flat stomach was visible for he had not yet zipped up his chinos. A wicked little spiral of heat twisted up from her pelvis. He was just so breathtakingly fanciable at every moment of the day.

Without any thought of what she was doing, she got up on her knees and pressed her lips to his stomach.

His hands came down in her hair and then he dropped down in front of her, eyes flashing molten gold over her pink face for she was embarrassed by her own boldness. He spread his fingers to her cheekbones ensuring she met his challenging gaze. 'Don't stop there, *ma belle*,' he murmured in a throaty tone of intimacy.

On the jolting journey back to the Anhara across the rough gravel plain that ringed the hills before the desert sands took over again, she was aware of the satisfied ache of her body and the indolent after-effects of their lovemaking, but even more conscious of the intense strength of her feelings for him. As he drove she rested a hand on his long, powerful thigh and occasionally he would cover her fingers with his own in an acknowledgement of her need to retain that closeness.

'We're happy,' she said softly.

'So we are,' Jaspar conceded lazily.

'Was it like this with you and Sabirah?' she heard herself ask, and she could have sworn that no thought of asking such a question had occurred to her, yet those impulsive words emerged from her lips nonetheless.

The silence fell like a curtain.

His surprised withdrawal was palpable in that brief silence and she could have kicked herself.

'Naturally not,' Jaspar finally responded with a perceptible lack of expression. 'We only met in company.'

In actuality, Freddy had not been referring to anything that related to physical intimacy for he had already told her that he and Sabirah had not been lovers. She had been referring to the sense of closeness and understanding that she herself felt with him and asking rather foolishly if he had felt the same with Sabirah. However, as he appeared only to think of *their* bonds in the most primitive of male sexual terms, yammering on about her own far more highflown sensations would be like laying her love at his wretched feet! She was furious with herself and with him.

'But times are changing. Career women in the city are beginning to go out in mixed social groups, but in rural areas and in conservative families parents are still very careful of their daughters' reputations.'

'When you want to change the subject, you don't need to give me a cultural lecture to do it!' Freddy snatched her hand from his muscular thigh as though he had slapped her.

'What's the matter?' Jaspar demanded.

'Nothing.' Face rigid, two high spots of hurt and chagrined colour marking her cheekbones, Freddy stared out through the dusty windscreen, watching the blinding sunlight begin to drain the desert sands of all colour and life. The hottest part of the day was approaching, which was why they had come out early and enjoyed brunch rather than lunch, for in another hour the temperature would scorch even in the shade.

Yet she still loved Quamar. It was a really beautiful country and the people were wonderfully friendly and welcoming. Jaspar had taken her out on lots of tours and tagging along with a male whom the Quamaris seemed to regard as being next door to a divinity had been educational. She had drunk goat's milk in nomadic tents, cheered at an impromptu horse race out in the desert and enjoyed chilled mint tea in the fashionable villas belonging to Jaspar's friends. And everywhere, no matter whom he was with and no matter how rich or humble his host, Jaspar was the same relaxed, courteous and charming guest, who always said and did the right thing.

'You're my wife. You have no reason to be jealous of my past,' Jaspar murmured drily.

'When your past arranges herself naked on your bed, I

have *every* reason!' Freddy flared, losing her temper with a suddenness that shook even her.

'It's unworthy of you to mention that episode. I hope you didn't gossip about that with Hasna as well,' Jaspar delivered in icy reproof, finally revealing that he had known all along that his niece had been the source of her identification of Sabirah.

'I didn't gossip with Hasna at all!' Freddy launched back furiously.

'But you *listened*,' Jaspar countered without skipping a beat.

She wanted to hit him for facing her with that unarguable point. 'Just stop this blasted car and let me out!'

'Don't be foolish. We're in the desert,' Jaspar murmured in the most infuriatingly superior tone.

Recognising that Jaspar wanted to protect Sabirah from the consequences of her escapade hurt Freddy and hardened her attitude. Surely the servants must have talked about the brunette's behaviour? How else had Hasna known that her father's widow had come to the Anhara that day to wait for Jaspar? So how dared Jaspar tell her that she shouldn't even mention that episode? Had theirs been a normal marriage from the outset, he would have had to give her a much more extensive explanation at the time.

'I would still like to know what you're arguing with me about,' Jaspar stated about fifteen minutes of unbroken silence later.

'You don't *want* to know.' And Freddy said not one more word during that drive.

Ben, who had spent the morning with his grandfather at the royal palace, was waiting in the hall to greet them, eager to show off his new drum set. He never returned without a gift and was generally overtired, overexcited and stuffed far too full of sweets as well. But Freddy had had to rethink her assumption that King Zafir's interest in his grandson might only be a whim for the older man spent time with Ben every week. Yet King Zafir had made no effort whatsoever to meet his son's new wife, Freddy reflected uneasily, wounded by that obvious and deliberate oversight.

As Ben ran to Jaspar, Jaspar swept him up and asked him in slow, distinct Arabic if he had had a good time. His nephew responded quite naturally in the same language and Freddy was unable to follow every word for she was learning at the slower rate of an adult. Although she had asked the staff to correct her mistakes, Jaspar had explained to her that all Quamaris would regard such an act as discourteous and that only a teacher would be relaxed in such a role with her, so Basmun had since been looking out for someone to instruct her in Arabic.

'I have a meeting. I must change,' Jaspar murmured.

Retrieving Ben, Freddy went off with Basmun to see how the work on the design for the new kitchens was coming on. She had learned a lot about historic buildings over the past month, not least that the Anhara might be their home and in the private ownership of the royal family but that Jaspar believed that no major changes should be considered without full consultation with the Department of National Monuments. Freddy had soon grasped that the best solution was simply to create new kitchens in some less historic part of the Anhara.

She checked over the plans with the architect and made an adjustment or two on Basmun's shyly proffered advice. By then it was lunchtime, but Ben was not hungry and moreover he was ready for a nap, so Freddy took him upstairs to his nanny. She was a lovely young woman with a bubbly sense of humour and not quite as given to spoiling Ben as the maids were. Ben cried for his teddy bear which was missing from his cot and Freddy realised that it must have been left in the gardens first thing that morning when she had seen Ben off on his visit to his grandfather.

'I'll get it. I know where it is,' Freddy assured the younger woman.

As she walked below the beautiful trees outside, sheltering from the heat of the sun, she thought over the silly argument she had had with Jaspar. It *had* been silly for she would have been disgusted had Jaspar been the sort of male who wanted the world to know that a woman had given him the kind of invitation that Sabirah had. And, furthermore, hadn't she herself been rather lacking in compassion over that whole episode? Wasn't it possible that, while grieving for her husband and feeling lonely and isolated within a family that did not seem to like her very much, Sabirah had done something crazy that she had just as swiftly regretted?

Having retrieved the missing teddy, Freddy had reached the junction of two paths when she saw an elderly white-bearded man standing below the trees. Clad in the sombre traditional dark blue robes worn by the desert herdsmen, he was leaning heavily on a stick and struggling with some difficulty to catch his breath in the hot, still air. He looked as if he was about to collapse and as she hurried towards him she noticed his lined features were grey and damp with perspiration.

'Come and sit down,' Freddy indicated the bench nearby and she cupped his elbow to demonstrate her meaning with action for she had little hope that he would understand English.

Taken aback, the older man protested in Arabic, which only increased his breathing difficulties. 'Please don't get upset,' Freddy begged. 'I'm only trying to help. You're not well and you really must rest. Did you walk all the way up the steps from the entrance gates? Those steps are very steep. I can hardly manage them myself.'

Freddy pressed him with determined hands down onto the seat. 'Breathe slowly,' she urged anxiously. 'I'm going to run indoors and fetch you a nice cold drink. Now, don't you dare move an inch or I'll be very cross with you.'

He gave her a shaken look from beneath his beetling white brows. His mouth opened.

'No, don't try to speak. Just rest until I come back.' Freddy sped back indoors. Finding Basmun hovering in the foyer, she told him that a doctor might be required because an elderly man had taken ill in the gardens. She then poured a glass of water from the cooler kept in a side porch for the benefit of thirsty staff and visitors and hurried back outside again.

On her breathless return, she was relieved to find the old man still seated where she had left him. With his hair and his beard and his quaint air of stately calm, he might have walked right out of the pages of the Bible. He accepted the glass of water and drank with appreciation before saying, 'Thank you. You are kind.'

'You look better,' Freddy remarked before it dawned on her that he had responded in her own language, and then she smiled in relief. 'I'm glad you speak English. I'm afraid I still only have a few words of Arabic, and when I first saw you I forgot every one of them! Are you here alone?'

'My…' he hesitated '…companions await me at the gates.'

'I think you should see a doctor.' Feeling very hot and bothered on her own account, Freddy waved a cooling hand in front of her face.

'I have seen too many doctors,' he complained, his fiercely intelligent dark eyes revealing his frustration. 'I am tired of being told to rest.'

'But resting is part of the healing process and you really ought to do as you're told. You mustn't neglect your health,' Freddy persisted gently.

'Are you in the habit of issuing orders to your visitors?'

'Only the stubborn ones.' But her usual bright smile was

weak for she was beginning to appreciate that she was not feeling at all well herself. 'I'm sorry...' she began, rising upright on legs that felt like wobbly sticks, her head swimming with sick dizziness, and a split second later she did something that she had never done before: she fainted.

CHAPTER NINE

FREDDY surfaced feeling woozy. She was lying on the bed in the air-conditioned cool of their room and Jaspar was staring down at her, his lean, dark features taut with concern.

He gripped her hand. 'My father's personal physician, Dr Kasim, is waiting outside to see you.'

'But I don't need to see a doctor,' Freddy muttered in embarrassment. 'I was silly. I went running about in that awful heat—'

'Fetching drinks of water for an obstinate man, who should have known better,' Jaspar interposed with a distinct lack of charity. 'My father is as anxious as I am to be assured that you have received a proper medical examination. You may have picked up a fever.'

While Freddy was striving dizzily to work out what possible connection King Zafir could have to the drink of water she had delivered to the old man in the gardens, Jaspar was already opening the door to another even more elderly gentleman with a clipped goatee beard. Jaspar looked inclined to hover, but Freddy raised a suggestive brow and he took the hint and left the room. She could see that he was really worried about her and she was touched, but she was mortified by the fuss that was being made.

Dr Kasim was the last word in tact. After answering his stream of questions and submitting to a minor examination, Freddy watched him write out his notes with punctilious care. He was so ancient, so stooped with venerable age, that she believed that she could hear his finger bones creaking.

'There's nothing wrong with me…is there?' she prompted.

'No, nothing wrong.' He looked up with a reassuring smile. 'You are in the early stages of pregnancy. I'm honoured to make that diagnosis and to be the first to give you that news.'

Freddy's soft lips parted and then slowly closed again. She was going to have a baby? Yes, that possibility had crossed her mind, but not in any serious way, more in a daydreaming fashion of what might be at some time in the future. Yet already their child had stolen a march on her expectations and taken life inside her. A wondering smile curved her mouth.

Dr Kasim cleared his throat. 'When you have engaged a gynaecologist, he will naturally advise you, but as you are at present my patient I would urge you to be very careful. Avoid exercise and anything which tires you. Drink only bottled water, eat only fresh food. Avoid spices and late nights and rest morning and afternoon…'

As his flood of instructions continued on beyond that point and included a pointed suggestion that all activity in the marital bed ought to cease forthwith as well, Freddy surveyed the wizened little doctor in growing disbelief. She was a healthy lump who rarely even caught a cold and he was talking to her as if she were a frail little flower. She found herself hoping that his strictures would ultimately prove to be several decades out of date.

'You cannot be too cautious when you carry a potential heir to the throne,' Dr Kasim informed her with great gravity. 'But as I am sure you wish to be discreet about that fact at present, be assured of my confidentiality.'

The joy of conception was a little dimmed for Freddy by the prospect of the sexless, spiceless eight months of early nights ahead of her, but she scolded herself for doubting the doctor's advice. After all, she thought mournfully,

Erica had not had an easy pregnancy. Her cousin had suffered from constant nausea. Freddy suppressed that unwelcome recollection and chose to concentrate instead on more uplifting images of an adorable little baby boy or girl with Jaspar's hair and Jaspar's wonderful smile...

He would be really pleased when she told him, yet she found herself reluctant to immediately share the news of her pregnancy. She would see a gynaecologist before she risked telling Jaspar that she was to be an untouchable couch potato for the foreseeable future. She was sure he would adhere to all such advice for Dr Kasim's sober words had impressed on her that the tiny being inside her womb could well end up being a king some day. But the more she considered the doctor's strictures, the more she wondered fearfully if he had noticed something during his examination that had suggested that she might be at risk of a miscarriage.

Yet here she and Jaspar were in the virtual honeymoon phase of their marriage and suddenly all that free and easy self-indulgence would have to stop... There would be no more nude bathing in the hills, no more wildly exciting encounters in the bed or the shower or on picnic rugs. Yes, she wanted their baby, but she was very much afraid that such severe limitations would damage their relationship.

'Why are you crying?' Jaspar's dark drawl startled her out of her frantic ruminations. He came down on the side of the bed and lifted her into his arms. 'Dr Kasim says you're fine...'

'Yes...' Freddy said in a wobbly voice, burying her damp, discomfited face in his shoulder, drinking in the familiar soothing scent of him and loving the feel of his arms around her. 'What age is he?'

'Must be eighty if he's a day, but my father has a great regard for him. A couple of younger doctors do make up his team. I thought you'd prefer an older man, *ma belle*,'

Jaspar murmured gently, smoothing the curly hair tumbling down her taut spine. 'Was I wrong?'

'He was very nice,' she conceded.

'You should be smiling. With a simple glass of water you have won my father's approbation. He is downstairs quoting the story of the Good Samaritan to the entire staff. I understand that you bullied him into sitting down and scolded him,' Jaspar drawled in a slightly charged under-tone.

Freddy emerged from the cover she had taken against his shoulder, aquamarine eyes shattered. 'Are you telling me that that elderly man outside was your father...the *King*?'

'He doesn't like helicopters and he was driven here. At the gates, he told his attendants that he would manage the steps up through the gardens without assistance and of course they dared not disobey him. I gather that he was in some distress when you spotted him—'

'Yes...' Freddy was aghast at the familiar way in which she had behaved towards his royal parent. 'Jaspar, I had no idea! He was dressed just like one of the tribesmen, like a shepherd—'

'He would soon tell you that he does not consider him-self in any way superior to the most humble of his sub-jects.' Jaspar's dark golden eyes were brimming with vi-brant amusement. 'He is so accustomed to being recognised that it didn't occur to him that such a misapprehension might arise.'

'My goodness, what a dreadful impression I must have made on him!' Freddy groaned in despair.

'Far from it. He was *very* impressed. Instead of calling for the servants, you took personal care of him and put yourself out on his behalf. He said you were a plain-speaking and charitable young woman and full of good sense. From him that is the highest of accolades. That you also look like a live angel may have helped him to swallow his loss of dignity.'

Colouring at that reference to angels, Freddy shook her blonde head for she was still in shock. 'I'm so grateful that I didn't offend him. But you don't expect to find a king wandering about all on his own in a garden and dressed just like he was anybody!'

Jaspar burst out laughing. 'I'll warn him to wear his crown on his next visit!'

'Stop it...' Freddy said, hot-cheeked with chagrin.

'My father has a great fondness for the Anhara because he once lived here with my mother. As you know she died when I was eighteen, but he misses her almost as much now as he did then. I suspect that he dismissed his attendants today because he wished to spend a few moments of private reflection in the gardens.'

'He must've loved her a great deal.'

'She was French on her mother's side and always spoke French in preference to Arabic. They were very well matched. She had a very definite personality.' Jaspar paused and gave her strained face a concerned appraisal. 'I *should* have taken you to meet my father weeks ago. But his moods have been so uncertain of late that I was afraid—'

'You were afraid that I might offend him.' Her throat closed over.

'I underestimated *both* of you and for that I owe you an apology. Do you think you will be feeling well enough to join us for dinner?'

Freddy gave him a valiant nod of confirmation for she was actually fighting to conceal the fact that she was on the brink of tears. She knew that she was in an over-sensitive mood and that her emotions were swimming about far too close to the surface, but she could not prevent herself from reading deeper meanings into what he had said:

they were *not* well matched as his parents had been. He had backed off from the challenge of letting her even meet his father…he had been ashamed of her.

And why shouldn't he be? Wasn't it time she faced up to a painful fact or two? Jaspar *should* have married a princess, an aristocrat or at the very least a well-born Quamari woman, who would have instinctively known how to behave in all sorts of situations. Freddy was painfully convinced that, but for King Zafir whimsically deciding to be impressed rather than insulted by her attitude towards him, she might have offended the older man for life and caused Jaspar great embarrassment and discomfiture.

Jaspar caught her coiled fingers in his and slowly unlaced them. 'I'm grateful that my father had the opportunity to meet you as your natural self.'

Her natural self? Outspoken, thoughtless, bossily barging in where angels feared to tread, Freddy translated, in no mood to be comforted by such words of support. She was a walking disaster and she had better hope that if their baby was a boy he took after Jaspar rather than her. 'We're together for ever, aren't we?' she muttered tightly.

Jaspar settled her carefully back against the pillows and stared down at her with a questioning intensity that she could feel, his stunning eyes narrowed. He looked distinctly pale at the prospect.

'Stuck together like salt and pepper…Ben and sex the only glue,' she framed chokily and stuffed her face in the pillows.

'That's *not* how I feel.' Jaspar swore in a raw undertone to her rigidly turned back. 'Don't talk like that. What's wrong? Did Dr Kasim upset you in some way?'

Silence answered him.

'I'm sorry I was sarcastic earlier,' Jaspar breathed abruptly, rather like a male mentally fingering through all potential sins.

'Why shouldn't you have been?'

'I hurt your feelings, *ma belle*.'

Now who was being tactless? Freddy's body language took on an even closer resemblance to a graven image carved in solid stone.

'Yet you only asked a harmless question,' Jaspar conceded flatly. 'But I'm willing to talk about Sabirah if you want. If I was uncomfortable before, it was only because I have never discussed that period of my life with anybody.'

The original man of steel and he was ready to tell all. But was she strong enough to hear the story of how much he had adored Sabirah without succumbing to an attack of low self-esteem that could take her a lifetime to recover from? It would make her feel insecure, encourage her to indulge in pointless comparisons between herself and the love of his life. *He* was the love of *her* life and dwelling on the past and what could not be changed was unhealthy and immature.

'I don't want to know about her...not *anything*,' Freddy told him with gloom-laden emphasis.

Silence lay again for several seconds while he attempted to comprehend her sudden change of heart.

'But—'

'I don't care in the slightest,' Freddy added thinly. 'Listening to blokes moaning about how they would never love again used to be one of the most tedious aspects of being single. I really don't think I ought to encourage you along the same path—'

'Freddy...' Jaspar growled, settling his hands to her waist to turn her over to face him again.

'Just you keep your inner feelings and thoughts to yourself. A stiff upper lip, we call it in England,' Freddy informed him with dogged conviction. 'Much the best attitude. Take your regrets to the grave with you, don't share them with me.'

Shimmering dark golden eyes clashed with hers. 'Message received.'

It was extraordinary. The minute she removed the pressure for him to talk about what he had most definitely not wanted to talk about, he behaved as if he had been rudely denied a welcome opportunity. He was furious with her volte-face. But Freddy was really grateful that she had seen the error of her ways. If Jaspar got talking about Sabirah, he would be *thinking* of the beautiful brunette and reliving the powerful emotions of the past. Did she really want to encourage such dangerous recollections? No, she did not indeed. Particularly not when it came to a female ready to strip off to capture him.

'But that won't prevent me from questioning you about every boyfriend you have ever had,' Jaspar announced, smooth as silk, rising up to his full height.

'The first one took me out because Erica bribed him to do it and the second one dumped me for her. After that, I was more cautious. There were a couple of brief entanglements. There was the guy who burst out crying over dinner talking about his ex-wife...' Freddy recalled, beyond all embarrassment. 'There was the one who brought his ex-girlfriend to visit so that she could explain that his talking to *me* about his feelings for *her* had helped them to get back together again—'

Jaspar was nailed to the spot, fascination stamped in his darkly handsome features. 'You're not serious, *ma belle*.'

'The virtually empty pages of my past experience with men contain few funny punchlines,' Freddy informed him flatly. 'They all without exception told me I was a very nice person but either they bored me to death or they were forever talking about the woman they really wanted who *didn't* want them.'

'That is not the case with us—'

'You had no choice, Jaspar. I blackmailed you into marrying me.'

'I can't say that there haven't been compensations.' Jaspar shot her a gleaming look of pure erotic recollection, his beautiful mouth curving into a wicked smile.

Her heart jumped up and down behind her breastbone and the little flame that never quite went out in his radius surged but, although she reddened, she looked stonily back at him.

'I think I should bale out of this conversation before I crash and burn beyond recovery,' Jaspar murmured drily.

The door closed behind him. Her mouth trembled but she buttoned it flat again. Had she mentioned the baby, how different things might have been, but once again she would have known that something other than her own self was keeping him with her. Not just Ben any more, but their own child as well. She loved Jaspar more than she had known she could ever love anybody, but she could not bear the idea that, in spite of all his caring gestures, she was so very much less than he had wanted in a wife. Even so, she knew that she would have to come to terms with the hurt to her pride and learn to appreciate what she did have.

An early dinner staged with King Zafir at the head of the imposing dining table and his entire entourage encamped on their knees in the hall beyond was something of a strain. He shot a string of questions at her without hesitation, established that she had a good working knowledge of the Bible and commented freely on her less detailed answers. In an effort to shield her, Jaspar stepped in once or twice, only to be told that he ought not to get into the habit of being a domineering husband who imagined his wife could not speak up for herself. A short and pithy lecture on the most important aspects of a successful marriage followed and Freddy marvelled at Jaspar's ability to sit through it with a straight face.

She was able to relax more and observe when the dialogue between father and son moved to more official matters, and she decided then that the older man was not quite as advanced in years as she had thought and was probably only in his late sixties. He was a strong character, not the type to suffer fools or indeed ill health with patience, but, in spite of his crusty and critical nature, he seemed to have an essentially kind heart. However, just listening, she was discovering where Jaspar had learned his rock-solid self-discipline: it had been forged in the fire of personal experience.

At the end of the meal, she read Jaspar's almost imperceptible signal that she ought to leave them alone and she wandered across the hall into the library, which had a large selection of English books, and sat down to read. Only forty minutes later, Jaspar appeared in the doorway, tall and dark and breathtakingly handsome in his tailored suit.

'I'm sorry I was in such a natty mood earlier,' she said straight off. 'Has your father left?'

'Yes. He was tired. I was proud of you,' he murmured levelly. 'You didn't allow him to intimidate you. He means well but his manner can be…'

'Abrasive?' she slotted in with her ready smile.

'Yes.' Stunning dark golden eyes rested on her, his lean, strong face rather taut. 'A month ago you asked me to make enquiries on your behalf and I did so. This afternoon, I received a report on your background that clarifies the matters which had concerned you.'

Freddy's eyes had widened and then she moved forward with eagerness. 'Oh, let me see it.'

'I took the liberty of reading it and I should warn you that it contains information which will upset you,' Jaspar advanced with measured care.

Freddy stilled in bewilderment. Upset her? Jaspar settled a folded document down on the coffee-table. Freddy stared at it and then in a sudden movement she stooped and snatched it up, shaking it open with visible impatience. Within the space of a minute, however, she was fumbling her way dizzily down onto the sofa behind her while she read and re-read only the first couple of sentences.

'This can't be true…this says that my mother died only ten years ago,' Freddy whispered incredulously.

'There is no question of a mistake this time. A copy of your mother's death certificate came with the report,' Jaspar informed her ruefully. 'But I don't understand *how* your late father found it possible to maintain the fiction that she had died when you were a baby.'

'He hated talking about her, but I put that down to his grief over her death, so I felt guilty when I asked him questions,' Freddy said unevenly. 'I'm so shocked that he lied to me…but it wasn't really that difficult for him to fool me—'

'How wasn't it difficult?' Jaspar prompted.

'He changed jobs and moved to the other end of the country soon after her supposed death. He said Mum had had no relatives left alive. In all my life, I never met anyone who had known her. When I asked for photographs and things like that…' her voice quivered '…Dad said the box containing the albums had gone missing during the house move. Ruth suspected that he'd been so devastated by my mother's death that he had burnt everything in a fit of grief.'

'He was a middle-aged bachelor when he met and married your mother and she was a good deal younger. Such inequal marriages often run into trouble.'

Freddy was reading the report but already foreseeing what was coming next. It *had* been her mother who had run off with another man. Yet she could hardly concentrate. Her mind was stuck on the awful realisation that her mother had not only abandoned her as a baby, but had also failed to make any attempt to regain contact with her daughter in all the years that had followed.

'She could never have loved me...she must have been like Erica...detached...' Freddy's strained voice petered out entirely as she absorbed the next section of the report. Indeed, so great was her disbelief, a strangled gasp escaped her. Her mother had given birth to twin girls shortly before she had left her father!

'I have sisters...that's not possible!' Freddy exclaimed vehemently.

Jaspar removed the document she was crushing between her fingers and came down beside her, enclosing a supportive arm to her rigid spine. 'Your father was convinced that the little girls were not his and when your mother took off with her latest lover he refused to accept responsibility for them. The babies were still in hospital at the time and the authorities took charge of them.'

'My s-sisters...' Freddy mumbled shakily. 'I have sisters and I never knew. How could Dad keep that from me?'

'Enquiries are still being made, but it won't be a simple matter to trace your sisters if they were adopted, as such very young children most likely were.' Jaspar expelled his breath in a rueful hiss.

'Mum deserted all of us. Cuckoos do that,' Freddy muttered with a shaken little laugh of acknowledgement. 'They leave their eggs in other bird's nests so that they don't have to be bothered with the work of raising them. Dad would have felt so humiliated. No wonder he moved hundreds of miles away afterwards. He would've hated people knowing the truth.'

'It's clear that your mother was a rather unstable personality—'

'You mean she had mental problems?' Freddy snatched up the report again and scanned the remaining information. 'There's no need to take refuge in euphemisms, Jaspar. She liked men a lot, by the looks of it, and there's nothing at all here about how she lived for the last twelve years of her life—'

'The enquiries are continuing. The agent believes that she may have changed her name or remarried at some stage, but by the time of her death she was living alone.'

'I suppose that's how you end up when you keep on abandoning other people.' Her face pale and stiff, Freddy tossed the report aside as if it meant nothing to her and stood up. 'I'm tired. Thank you for getting that information for me.'

'Freddy...don't be too hard on your father for keeping you in the dark. He probably believed that he was protecting you,' Jaspar murmured.

Freddy compressed her lips. 'Maybe.'

'Don't beat yourself up about this, *ma belle*.' He tugged her into the circle of his arms. 'What bearing does your background really have on your life now?'

Freddy looked up at him with helpless hostility. Jaspar with his six hundred years of ancestral history and the solid family tree that the whole al-Husayn family revered. There was no chance that he would ever suffer the sense of deep humiliation and betrayal that she was attempting to conceal from him.

'I appreciate that you think it's easy for me to make such a statement,' Jaspar persisted, his fabulous cheekbones scored with faint colour. 'But you are who you are.'

As unloved by her mother as her poor sisters had been from birth. And the father she had trusted had thought too much of his own pride to tell her the truth. She turned her head away, swallowing hard.

'We'll find your sisters. It may take a while but it *can* be done,' Jaspar asserted.

'Yeah...' Freddy nodded jerkily and broke away from

him before the tears thickening her throat got the upper hand.

Upstairs, she locked herself in the bathroom, ran a bath and had a good cry while the water was running. She was reeling in shock from what she had learned and it was little wonder that she felt gutted for she had had a very idealised image of her mother. Now that innocent image had been smashed for all time.

She pretended to be asleep when Jaspar came to bed.

'I'll be leaving tomorrow for three days. I have to attend a meeting in Dubai in my father's stead,' Jaspar announced as he undressed in the darkness, evidently unimpressed by her efforts to fake slumber. 'I wish you could have accompanied me but the last thing you need right now is the stress of making polite chit-chat to complete strangers—'

'And then you doubt I could even manage that,' Freddy put in thinly.

'If you can cope with my father, you are more than equal to any challenge.'

'Tell me…are you always this relentlessly charming in the face of adversity?'

'I know you're hurting right now and that there is really nothing I can do to alter that. I was tempted to destroy that report and tell you that the agent had come up with nothing of a new or mysterious nature…but you had the right to know the truth and I honour my promises.'

'I married a saint.'

The mattress gave with his weight and almost simultaneously he reached for her. He stole the breath from her body with a hungry kiss. 'Stop trying to fight with me.'

He was strong and warm against her, the heat of his lean, muscular frame defrosting the lonely chill inside her heart. And when he kissed her, her rebellious body came alive with feeling and longing and love. She could have bitten out her tongue for being so ungracious and unpleasant to him. Why she should continually attack him when he had shown her only understanding she had no idea, but she was ashamed. She shifted into him, adoring the scent and the touch of him.

'I get irritated with you being so perfect all the time,' she muttered in a small voice.

Jaspar laughed huskily. 'I'm far from perfect and you know it—'

'You're a darned sight more perfect than I am...' He was extracting her from the nightdress she had donned as something of a statement with the kind of smooth expertise that took her breath away. 'I mean, when and where did you learn to do this, for a start?'

'No comment. Sometimes you ask the craziest questions, *ma belle*,' Jaspar muttered thickly, running an explorative hand over the swell of her full breasts, lingering to tease at a straining peak and provoking a low moan from deep in her throat.

Her back arched, a dulled ache throbbing between her thighs, and she was instantly, wantonly and irretrievably on fire for him. All the stress she had endured seemed to find a vent in that fierce surge of desire. But a moment later she recalled the doctor's advice and, dismayed that she could have so easily forgotten that warning, she jerked back from Jaspar as if she had been burnt.

'No...we can't...'

Jaspar uttered a short succinct word that she had never heard before, but she needed no translation to know that it was a curse word.

'Jaspar...'

'I've had enough,' Jaspar breathed with thunderous quietness, and he tossed back the sheet and got out of bed again.

In the moonlight, he was a lithe silvered shadow. Aghast

at his departure, Freddy sat up and exclaimed, 'I'm sorry, I—'

'Forget it,' he said with dark satire as he pulled on a pair of jeans.

'Where are you going?'

'Freddy—'

'Can I come too?'

'That would rather defeat the point, wouldn't it?'

'I just don't want you to go,' she admitted chokily.

'Give me a break. One minute you're pushing me away as if I'm assaulting you, and the next you're begging me to stay?'

'*Please*...'

The silence buzzed with his fierce reluctance; she could feel it.

'Sorry...' Jaspar opened the door. 'I just want a good night's sleep.'

'It wasn't that I didn't want you,' she began in a rush. 'It's just that I'm...I'm pregnant!'

But the door closed with a thud at the exact same time as she spoke and there was no way he could have heard her. For a whole hour afterwards, she hated herself. Of course, he didn't understand why she had reacted like that, but she had inflicted too many of her see-sawing emotions on him and he had reached saturation point. She got out of bed, retrieved her nightdress and went off to look for him. He was fast asleep in a bedroom two doors down from their own, no sheet over him, no air-conditioning on, not even the curtains closed.

From the foot of the bed she surveyed him and tears made her eyes feel all hot and prickly. She had never really understood how vulnerable love would make her until she looked at Jaspar asleep and her heart just threatened to break inside her because she was terrified of losing what they had. Crowding him, she decided ruefully, was not a good idea. With a last lingering look at the bold profile etched against the pale linen and the long elegant sweep of his brown back, she tiptoed back out again.

She rose early the next morning to have breakfast with him before he left and found Ben, beaming and still in his pyjamas, keeping Jaspar company. Sheathed in a charcoal-grey business suit of exquisite cut, he looked breathtakingly handsome.

'If it's any consolation,' Jaspar confided with his charismatic smile, 'I had a lousy night's sleep.'

'I didn't do so well myself,' Freddy confided, heart singing that the awkwardness of the night before was behind them.

In the shelter of the outside porch, he drew her close to his lean, powerful body, stunning dark golden eyes intent on her, and claimed her mouth in a slow, searching kiss that left her every skincell humming.

'To be continued,' he murmured with husky sensuality.

Two days later, Freddy emerged smiling from her appointment with a consultant gynaecologist. She had been told that she was in excellent health and all her fears had been set to rest. Dr Kasim's strictures had indeed been judged rather too stringent. Her bodyguards awaited her on the ground floor of the ultra-modern hospital and as soon as the lift doors opened they moved forward, looking relieved by her reappearance. She suspected that Jaspar had instructed them to stick to her like superglue but, appreciating the amount of attention their presence would attract, she had asked them to stay downstairs. In about twelve hours, she thought happily, Jaspar would be with her again and she could hardly wait to tell him about their baby.

The limousine travelled through the wide tree-lined streets of the city and on to the royal palace. Jaspar had informed her that they had a large apartment within the massive palace complex and she was keen to see it. The palace was a sprawling weathered sandstone collection of buildings, the earliest of which dated back to the thirteenth century. As her visit had been prearranged, she was greeted at the main door by a little man who introduced himself as Rashad and who bowed so low to her that she was afraid that he might topple over.

It was soon evident that Rashad was acting on her father-in-law, King Zafir's instructions and that merely showing her the way to Jaspar's apartment was the least of them. Rashad had been asked to give her an official tour of the palace and instruct her on the history of the al-Husayn family. He was a very nice man, but after two solid hours of trekking up and down stairs, along endless corridors and through innumerable courtyards, Freddy began to feel rather tired. Catching a glimpse of her own wan face in a mirror, she suggested to her companion that perhaps they could continue the tour another day.

Rashad delivered her to the sunlit outer courtyard of what Jaspar had airily described as an apartment. Sheltering behind a glorious fountain and a very beautiful casuarina tree lay what Freddy would have described as a most substantial house. She smiled at the fabulous arrangement of yellow roses in the spacious hall, relished the air-conditioned cool and was taken aback when she was informed that a visitor already awaited her.

'A visitor?' she questioned, her heart sinking, for there was nothing she wanted more than to kick off her shoes, sit down and enjoy a relaxing cup of tea.

The senior manservant lowered his gaze. 'Princess Sabirah has been waiting for some time.'

Freddy tensed. Well, she supposed that, whether she liked it or not, the meeting was overdue. In recent weeks, she had received visits from Adil's eldest daughter, Medina, as well as Hasna's English mother, Genette, and her younger sisters. Each and every one of them had been charming and she had got on like a house on fire with Genette, who was very good-natured and friendly. Perhaps she herself had been remiss in not extending a polite invitation to Sabirah, she thought ruefully, for that ghastly embarrassing scene in which they had initially met at the Anhara *had* to be got over and sensibly forgotten: Sabirah was a member of Jaspar's family and could not be ignored.

In the sunlit drawing-room, which was furnished with mellow antiques, Sabirah rose to greet her and for a moment Freddy could do nothing but stare for Sabirah was *so* beautiful, far more stunning than Freddy had allowed herself to recall. The brunette had the perfection of an exquisite china doll and her fitted blue designer suit was a superb frame for her slender, elegant figure.

Instantly Freddy felt *huge* in comparison and she said awkwardly, 'I'm sorry I wasn't here when you arrived.'

'I'm relieved that you're willing to speak to me after the unfortunate way in which we first learnt of each other's existence.' Sabirah's smooth and unembarrassed reference to her own bold presence in Jaspar's bedroom on the same day that Freddy had married Jaspar increased rather than defused Freddy's tension. 'I'm willing to surrender my pride for Jaspar's sake.'

Freddy frowned. 'I beg your pardon?'

Exotic slanted dark eyes rested on her. 'I've come here to ask you to set Jaspar free.'

Freddy stared at the gorgeous brunette, her natural colour ebbing, her heart rate speeding up. 'That's...that's quite a major demand.'

'Jaspar loves me and I love him.' Sabirah spoke with daunting confidence. 'Perhaps that doesn't matter to you. Perhaps you don't care that he will never be happy with you. But Jaspar doesn't deserve to lose his one chance of happiness just because Adil fathered an illegitimate child.'

Freddy tensed even more. So Sabirah knew about Ben.

'You have no need to look dismayed. I don't resent the child. Why should I? I didn't love my husband,' Sabirah told her without hesitation. 'I only want to talk about Jaspar—'

'But I don't *want* to discuss Jaspar,' Freddy cut in tautly.

Sabirah's lustrous dark eyes hardened. 'I'm only asking you to *listen*.'

'Maybe I don't want to listen either,' Freddy could sit still no longer. Getting up, she walked across to the window and then looked back with pronounced reluctance at her unwelcome visitor, wondering if she could just ask her to leave. Part of her wanted to listen but the other part of her was more afraid of what she might hear.

'Jaspar and I fell in love almost six years ago,' Sabirah proclaimed. 'But we were discreet about our feelings for neither of us was in a hurry to marry.'

So Jaspar had never actually got as far as proposing to the brunette, Freddy interpreted from that statement. Strengthened by that suspicion, she said quietly, 'I'm not trying to rain on your parade but all this happened an awfully long time ago.'

Sabirah ignored that comment and Freddy flushed.

'As soon as Adil decided that *he* was in love with me, Jaspar and I were forced apart,' Sabirah stated emotively. 'My family put enormous pressure on me to accept Adil's proposal. As far as they were concerned it was a great honour and one day I would become queen of Quamar.'

As that scenario was exactly what Freddy had once imagined, she was dismayed for she did not want to think of Jaspar and Sabirah as star-crossed lovers, separated through no fault of their own.

'Only imagine my feelings when I later discovered that not only was my husband an appalling womaniser but also that he had *never* been destined to become king!' Sabirah acknowledged Freddy's look of surprise at that news with a grim little smile. 'During our honeymoon, Adil admitted that his father had informed him when Jaspar was only fifteen that Jaspar would succeed to the throne.'

'But Adil was Crown Prince,' Freddy muttered in disconcertion.

'His title was merely a convenient screen to allow Jaspar to grow up with greater freedom. Adil was content with the pretence,' Sabirah asserted with a shrug. 'He accepted that Jaspar had many fine qualities that he himself didn't have and he was not an ambitious man.'

Of course, it made much greater sense that Jaspar should all along have been the son intended for the throne, Freddy conceded inwardly. Adil with his three marriages and his taste for party girls would not have been a wise choice of ruler for a conservative country and her father-in-law was not a foolish man.

Sabirah leant forward in a confiding way. 'That's what I'm trying to explain to you. Jaspar will never be selfish. Jaspar will always put family loyalty before his own personal feelings.'

Freddy could not argue with that assessment and her heart sank right down to her toes for she knew exactly what Sabirah was building up to telling her.

'But don't you think that Jaspar deserves to be happy?' Sabirah demanded pointedly.

'Yes, of course I do, *but—*'

'Do you realise that Jaspar has not spoken one private word to me since the day I agreed to marry his brother? That's how loyal he was to his brother even though he loved me himself! I went to the Anhara that day in an effort to force him to declare his feelings for me—'

'Jaspar doesn't respond very well to force,' Freddy slotted in tightly, her tummy churning. If there was a word of truth in Sabirah's passionate argument, it meant that she herself was hanging onto a marriage that was doomed, for with Sabirah on the sidelines how could her own relation-ship with Jaspar ever grow? He would always be thinking back to what might have been and eventually bitterness would set in.

'Jaspar adores me but he is too conscious of his position to ask you for a divorce. But if *you* were to leave *him*, he would be granted a divorce and he would then be free to marry me without attracting criticism.'

'I wouldn't marry you if you were the last woman left alive in Quamar,' Jaspar imparted with stinging derision from the doorway, startling both Sabirah and Freddy to such an extent that they spun round to gape at him.

Sabirah went rigid. 'Of course you will say that in your wife's presence, for you don't want to hurt her, but—'

'Do you realise how long I've been standing outside this room listening?' Jaspar demanded, brilliant golden eyes shimmering, lean, dark face clenched hard as he studied the woman proclaiming herself to be the one and only love of his life. 'Let me tell you that I found the Romeo and Juliet slant to your colourful tale nauseous!'

While wondering what on earth Jaspar was doing back a full ten hours ahead of what he had assured her to be a most rigid schedule, Freddy had never been more relieved to hear so blunt a speech of rebuttal. Two high spots of red now burned over Sabirah's cheekbones. Aghast at Jaspar's inopportune appearance, Sabirah had been silenced. But what shook Freddy the most was her recognition of the icy rage barely leashed in Jaspar's lancing appraisal of the tiny brunette. Even the most disinterested observer would have realised that Jaspar had the utmost contempt for the other woman.

'Your own father *begged* you not to marry Adil. He thought the age gap between you was too great and, in despair at your determination to become a Crown Princess, your father finally told you that my brother would be an unfaithful husband.' Jaspar's evident inside knowledge of those facts made Sabirah shoot him a look of dismay. 'But your own ambition triumphed over all the warnings. How dare you try to destroy my marriage, which is as happy as your own was miserable?'

'How can you speak to me like this after what we were to each other?' Sabirah demanded shrilly, outraged pride stamped in her stunning face.

'I have long been grateful that Adil saved me from making the biggest mistake of my life. Now leave us,' Jaspar commanded. 'I suggest you enjoy a long vacation at your parents' country house—'

'I don't want to go home to my parents!' the brunette launched at him with unconcealed horror at the suggestion.

'It is my father's command and if you prefer to wait until he summons you to tell you *why* that is his wish, feel free to do so,' Jaspar advised silkily.

Sabirah paled to the colour of parchment and averted her eyes. She hurried out of the room without another word.

'I doubt if she will even stop to pack,' Jaspar murmured with grim satisfaction. 'She has only recently ended a rampant affair with a city businessman whose wife discovered them *in flagrante delicto*. Rumours are already circulating. Naturally she wishes to put a few thousand miles between herself and my father for he has lost all patience with her.'

'Sabirah's been having an affair?' Freddy exclaimed in sharp disconcertion. 'Even while she's been chasing after you?'

'Sabirah craves status and position above all else. How on earth she managed to convince herself that I would ever look at her with favour again, I have no idea.' Jaspar shook his dark head. 'She has a very much exaggerated concept of her own attraction.'

'She's incredibly beautiful...and you were awfully

shocked that day when you saw her on your bed. I'm sure that must have...er...upset you,' Freddy muttered tautly.

'Indeed it did. I was as embarrassed as a teenage boy. One doesn't want to see one's sister-in-law naked,' Jaspar countered with a grimace that was very eloquent. 'In my eyes, she will always be Adil's wife and I was appalled that she could be that shameless.'

'But you didn't want me gossiping about her. I assure you that I never breathed a word about that episode.'

'Freddy...I didn't want *anyone* gossiping,' Jaspar responded with an unexpected laugh. 'If any more wild rumours about Sabirah escape she will never attract a second husband. My whole family is praying that she will eventually remarry so that we will be free of her and what hope have we got if she destroys her reputation?'

Freddy surveyed him with bemused eyes. 'You don't feel anything at all for her...do you? I thought that she was supposed to be the love of your life.'

'She hurt my pride most. In my own way I was quite conceited five years ago,' Jaspar confided with deadly seriousness and a look of regret that squeezed her heart, for she suspected that her idea of conceit and his would not tally. 'Adil was twice her age and a very large man but she married him without hesitation.'

'But you loved her—'

'I *thought* I loved her but I now believe that it was more of a lust to possess than love. I didn't understand the difference then. I was humiliated by the discovery that she would sacrifice everything for ambition. I then had the very great advantage of seeing how she conducted herself as my brother's wife.' His strong jawline hardened. 'Watching her snub the family members whom she outranked and encourage malicious gossip for her own amusement killed any lingering regrets I had pretty fast.'

'Were you aware that your father *always* planned for you

to be his successor?' Freddy asked, yielding to her considerable curiosity on that point.

'I had not the faintest idea until he told me so last week. I marvel that Adil did not hate me for it,' Jaspar confessed. 'I finally understand why my brother made no effort to reform his lifestyle. I also believe that the disappointment of learning that she would never become queen twisted Sabirah into the hard, bitter woman that she has since become.'

Recognising his faint pity for the brunette, Freddy let go of her last fear that he still cherished Sabirah in some corner of his heart, and so intense was her relief that she felt a little dizzy and she sank down heavily onto a sofa.

Jaspar crossed the room so fast that he might have been a bullet fired from a gun. Crouching down by her side, he breathed in a driven undertone, 'We have wasted all this time talking about Sabirah but tell me now without further delay, what is the matter with you?'

Her brows pleated. She studied him, read the strain in his lean, darkly handsome features, the pallor stamped beneath his bronzed skin, the clear anxiety in his searching dark golden gaze. 'I don't know what you're talking about.'

'I know you were at the hospital this morning and that when your bodyguards saw you again you were very pale and serious,' Jaspar recounted tautly.

Freddy's frown increased. 'You've been spying on me!'

'I just *need* to know what's wrong with you. I cancelled my last meeting in Dubai and flew home. I've been worried sick. And then I arrived back and find that witch telling you a pack of nonsensical lies!' Jaspar groaned.

'I'm not ill. I can tell you that much.' Freddy veiled her dancing eyes but she was touched by the level of concern he was making no attempt to hide from her.

Jaspar studied her in bewilderment. 'If you weren't ill, why were you at the hospital?'

'I'm pregnant.'

'You're not ill?' Jaspar prompted like a record stuck in a groove.

'Well, if I'd listened to Dr Kasim I would probably be considering myself next door to being a bedridden invalid,' Freddy said cheerfully. 'But I saw a consultant gynaecologist today and he was very reassuring. He says I'm a healthy pregnant woman.'

'You're expecting a baby…*already*?' Jaspar studied her with wondering dark golden eyes. 'But we've only been married a few weeks. That possibility didn't even cross my mind. You're actually going to have a baby.'

'Yes, I believe we've established that fact.' Freddy was tickled pink by his shock and the sort of reverent light beginning to glow in his gaze as he began to finally absorb what he was being told.

Jaspar scooped her bodily off the sofa and sank down with her on his lap, both arms wrapped round her. 'You've known since Dr Kasim saw you at the Anhara? Why didn't you tell me?'

'I wanted a second opinion. He told me we oughtn't even to sleep together any more,' Freddy admitted in a rueful rush. 'That's why I said no that night—'

'You can say no whenever you like. I acted like a fool.' Jaspar swore, closing one lean hand tightly over hers. 'I was trying to comfort you and, of course, making love was the last thing you felt like. Unfortunately, I couldn't resist my own urge to express my feelings for you in a more physical way. I'm sure I seemed insensitive to you, but it was not meant in that way.'

Freddy was quite flabbergasted by that confessional speech.

'Until this moment this has been a dreadful day, *ma belle*,' Jaspar admitted with a ragged edge to his dark, deep drawl. 'First I received the news of your mysterious hospital visit—'

'I don't see why that should have bothered you so much—'

'Initially it didn't, but then fear started to build at the back of my mind and I could not concentrate no matter how hard I tried. I began to imagine that all sorts of things might be wrong with you and I had to be with you, I *had* to come home.'

Freddy toyed with his silk tie. 'Silly,' she said, while loving every word he had spoken for his description of his mounting anxiety touched her heart to its core.

'So forgive me if I have not yet shown my pleasure at the news of our child's conception,' Jaspar urged. 'I'm still in shock. Are you sure you're in good health?'

'I'm *very* healthy,' Freddy told him with gentle emphasis.

His arms tightened round her. He bowed his proud dark head over hers and pressed her close. 'I was sick with worry. Our baby...that is wonderful news, but the knowledge that you are well still feels like the best news of all.'

She smoothed her fingertips over one strong cheekbone. He turned his mouth into her hand and kissed her palm.

'Three months before my mother died, she went for a simple check-up at the hospital and learned that she was terminally ill. She did not tell us until her condition could no longer be concealed and by then she had little time left to share with us. We always regretted that she couldn't trust us to be strong for her...' Jaspar muttered rather thickly. 'I have had a most irrational fear of hospitals ever since.'

Tears stung Freddy's eyes. She hugged him close, loving him all the more for sharing that sad little story with her and finally understanding why her intelligent and usually very sensible husband had overreacted to such an extent to the discovery that she had kept an appointment at the hospital.

'I can have the baby at home,' she told him soothingly.

'But that might not be safe and above all your safety is what counts, *ma belle*,' Jaspar intoned huskily. 'You know, I love you very much…'

As he lifted his head and she tipped up hers, she collided with a look more open and more intense than any she had yet received from him, and her heart jumped and she ran out of breath.

'At first, it was lust of the lowest order,' Jaspar confessed a little shamefacedly. 'And then it became obsessional lust. I never wanted any woman as much as I wanted you, but I was initially so angry at being pushed into marrying you that I did not recognise my own feelings.'

'You don't need to apologise for that.' Joy was spreading through Freddy in a heady flood.

'Even when I didn't want to be drawn to you, I was. I was intrigued when you stood up to me and I began to appreciate that you *did* love Ben. But I wasn't as generous as I ought to have been about the extent of your love for my nephew,' Jaspar murmured gruffly. 'By then, I wanted you to want me for myself, not because I was your ticket to possessing Ben. Initially that made me feel bitter and used.'

Freddy was stricken by that admission. 'I never dreamt that you felt like that—'

'But I couldn't stop thinking about you the whole time I was in New York and then I came home to discover that you were sleeping in the nursery and it was like a red rag to a bull!' Jaspar loosed a reluctant laugh. 'Ben seemed to have much more pulling power with you than I had, *ma belle*.'

'No, you always had pulling power,' Freddy assured him

feverishly, wrapping both arms round him to emphasise the point. 'I just started—'

A loud knock on the door finally penetrated their cocoon of mutual absorption.

'What the hell?' Jaspar groaned, setting her down more sedately on the seat beside him.

It was Rashad who entered with much apologetic bowing. He spoke in Arabic and Jaspar instantly rose to his feet looking puzzled.

'Your friend, Ruth, has phoned several times. I believe she has some urgent news she wishes to share with you,' he explained as Rashad withdrew again. 'I'm sorry. If I hadn't instructed the staff that we were not to be disturbed her call would have been put straight through to you.'

Freddy was perplexed. 'I can't imagine what Ruth could possibly have to tell me that would qualify as urgent.'

'You had better call her immediately.'

Freddy got up to do so, anxiously wondering what was wrong, for Ruth was not the kind of woman likely to employ the word urgent without good reason. She had written twice to the other woman, rather awkward communications for she had not yet managed to bring herself to the point of admitting that her marriage to Jaspar had become a real marriage.

'Freddy?' Ruth sounded unusually excited. 'Is that you?'

'Yes, it's me—'

'I have fantastic news for you!' the older woman asserted with satisfaction. 'You have the right to take Ben and come back to London with him.'

'Come back to London with Ben?' Freddy echoed, wide-eyed.

'I searched your cousin's apartment from top to bottom and I finally found her will—'

'Erica really *did* write a will?' Freddy queried in some surprise.

'I would've found it a lot sooner had I not foolishly
assumed that *you* had done a thorough search of her personal effects!' Ruth stated in frank reproof. 'Had you done
so, you could have saved yourself all this grief. Erica left
you *everything*!'

'Erica left me…what?'

'Everything she possessed as well as full legal guardianship of Ben. Have you nothing to say, Freddy?'

'I'm so shocked…' Meeting Jaspar's narrowed stare,
Freddy pressed the phone to her shoulder and murmured
shakily. 'Ruth's found Erica's will and my cousin left me
everything including guardianship of Ben…'

Tears thickened Freddy's voice and then overflowed,
dampening her cheeks. The knowledge that Erica had
trusted her to that extent *and* had taken the trouble to have
such a will drawn up had shaken her. Erica might not have
taken to motherhood, but she had cared enough about her
son to consider Ben's future in the event of anything happening to her.

'If I were you, I would just sneak back home with Ben
the minute you get the chance,' Ruth suggested. 'Legally,
the al-Husayn family can do nothing to prevent you from
keeping him.'

Freddy's thoughts were straying as she watched Jaspar
leave the room, his sculpted profile clenched and pale. 'I'm
pregnant, Ruth—'

'Say that again—'

'I fell madly in love with Jaspar and we're having a
baby,' Freddy extended in an apologetic tone. 'He's absolutely wonderful. I'm sorry I wasn't more honest in my
letters…and when you've made such an effort on my behalf
and found Erica's will, I feel awful.'

Freddy listened anxiously to the humming silence on
the line.

'I presume I can now look forward to regular holidays in a royal palace?' Ruth enquired.

'Oh, yes. We'd love to have you!'

'I'll forgive you.' Ruth laughed, but she sounded shattered for all that.

Finishing the call with a promise of phoning back later, Freddy went off to look for Jaspar. Why on earth had he left the room? His seeming pallor must have been a trick of the light, she decided, for Jaspar must surely have guessed that she had been on the very brink of telling him that she loved him before Rashad had interrupted them.

Jaspar had not gone far. He was pacing up and down the hall like a prowling tiger, every movement betraying his high-voltage tension. As soon as he heard her steps, he swung round, lean, powerful face clenched taut, dark golden eyes filled with pain. 'The minute I saw your tears of relief, I realised what was coming next. Now that you have a legal right to Ben and adequate resources, you want me to let you go because I have nothing further to offer you...'

Comprehension sank in on Freddy then.

'I *can't* do it. I can't let you go,' Jaspar swore vehemently. 'I can't imagine my life without you and Ben. These last weeks we have shared have been very precious to me. What must I do to convince you that if you give me enough time I can make you happy here in Quamar?'

'Jaspar—'

But Jaspar was too wound up to be silenced. 'I know you've been making the best of things for Ben's sake—'

'That's not true—'

'The last few weeks, I didn't care...it was enough for me—'

'Jaspar, will you let me get a word in and will you calm down?' Freddy launched at him in frustration. 'I love you! I haven't the slightest intention of asking you to let me go.

As for me having made the best of things with you...well, in one sense that *is* true. You're the best thing that ever happened to me and I fancied you like mad the minute I laid eyes on you.'

'Keep talking...' Jaspar encouraged, giving every impression of a male locked into her every word as he moved forward.

'I felt so guilty about having blackmailed you into marriage and then...well, being so *happy* with you seemed wicked and self-serving.'

'But I'm glad you blackmailed me into marriage—'

'You were ripping about it at the start,' Freddy reminded him helplessly.

'But I adapted fast,' Jaspar pointed out as he bent and swept her with great care up into his arms. 'I soon saw that you were the woman for me—'

'In bed, first of all,' Freddy slotted in.

'Are you telling me that you knew you *loved* me the first time we got between the sheets?'

Meeting that dubious downward look, Freddy reddened fiercely. 'No, but at least I didn't yammer on about it *only* being sex!'

'I knew those words would return to haunt me.' Shouldering shut the door of a spacious bedroom, Jaspar gave her a wolfish grin and settled her down on the canopied bed. 'But while I still believed that you had been my brother's woman first, I couldn't concede that the attraction was any stronger. You would have laughed yourself sick had you heard me only a couple of hours later fighting to *stay* married to you!'

'Fighting?'

'With my father. The first thing he said to me on the score of our marriage was that if I had married you on a foolish impulse, he would be doing me a kindness in having it set aside.' His dark golden eyes gleamed as he gazed

down at her with a warmth that felt like sunshine on her
rapt face. 'And no sooner had he spoken than I was gripped
by the most powerful need to hold onto you and it had
precious little to do with Ben—'

'Honestly?' Freddy prompted.

'Honestly.' Jaspar swept her carefully up into his arms.
'We've both used Ben as our excuse to be together. We
hid behind him when we weren't yet ready to face our
feelings for each other.'

'I knew pretty soon how I felt about you,' Freddy whispered.

'Tell me that you love me again,' Jaspar urged.

A glorious smile lit her face at his eagerness to hear those
words again for she wanted the exact same words. 'I love
you loads—'

'I adore you. How could you not realise how I felt about
you?'

'Because you're kind of a special person anyway,' she
told him feelingly. 'I just thought you were making a real
effort to ensure that our marriage worked.'

'I wanted you to love me—'

'Not when I called you a wimp, you didn't. That was
such an awful thing for me to throw at you.' Freddy sighed
with an excessive lack of tact.

'I *had* decided that I didn't want to fall in love again,'
Jaspar admitted rather grittily, colour demarcating his fabulous cheekbones. 'There was some grounds for you to
accuse me of using Sabirah as an excuse to think all women
were untrustworthy and out to get me—'

'Oh, they probably *were* out to get you.'

'But I have never treated any woman badly,' Jaspar intoned steadily. 'Except you—'

'If these last few wonderful weeks have been what you
call treating me badly, what is *good* treatment like? I can
hardly wait.' Freddy was quite unable to be serious. She

was so happy, she was on an unstoppable high. The man of her dreams, the father of her baby and her husband was studying her as though she was the most precious being in his world. For the first time, she felt that Jaspar was truly hers to love and her conscience troubled her no longer.

'I have the rest of my life to show you, *ma belle*,' Jaspar told her, smoothing a wondering hand over her still-flat tummy and splaying his long, lean fingers. 'Are we really going to have a baby?'

'Yes.'

'You're fantastic...'

'So are you.' She dragged him down to her and he took the hint and crushed her readily parted lips beneath his own with all the hunger she craved.

'Are you sure we should be doing this?' Jaspar surfaced to ask at one point, passion and concern mingled in his possessive gaze as he lay over her literally rigid with the effort self-control was demanding from him. 'I love you so much and I could not stand to risk your health in any way. Are you *really* sure?'

Freddy was awfully glad she had not let Dr Kasim within an inch of her impressionable husband. 'You can come and see the consultant with me the next time.'

Jaspar gave her his wonderful smile. 'That would make me feel better. But right now, all I need is to hold you and show you my love, *ma belle*.'

Freddy had no objections to that plan whatsoever and the rest of the afternoon melted away without either of them thinking about anything but their joy in each other.

In his own apartments a good quarter-mile away, King Zafir waited in vain for his son and his daughter-in-law to join him for lunch. Rashad insisted that he had passed on the invitation. His royal employer fretted and fumed at Jaspar and Freddy's lack of punctuality and wondered what on earth had got into Jaspar. Around then, the older man egan recalling the first months of his own happy marriage. n abstracted smile on his lined features, he ate his lunch nd uttered not another word of complaint.

st over a year later, Freddy strolled through the gardens f the Anhara with her younger son, Kareem, in his pram nd her elder son, Ben, riding his bike.

Ben was now entitled to call himself an al-Husayn as ell for she and Jaspar had adopted him the previous year. he still thrilled to the knowledge that Ben was now truly leir little boy. Ben might have lost out by the manner of is birth on being a prince but, as Jaspar had pointed out, le position carried many restrictions and a great deal of esponsibility. Ben would grow up free to make choices lat their younger son, Kareem, was unlikely to ever enjoy. lamed in honour of the very first King of Quamar, Kareem ould be raised just as Jaspar had been, to put his country rst, his family second and his own personal wishes last of ll.

Kareem was such an easy baby to look after, Freddy lought as she looked proudly down at her infant son whose ttle inner time clock already seemed to suggest a certain atural discipline. Kareem slept within minutes of being laced in his cot *and* through most of the night. One of aspar's aunts had told her that Jaspar had been like that s a baby too: calm and uncomplaining. But Freddy reckned that some babies instinctively knew and appreciated hen they were secure and loved.

Ben paused on his bike to peer down into the pram. Kareem's sleeping again,' he lamented. 'When will he lay with me?'

'Another couple of months and he'll be sitting up and a ttle more fun—'

'Will he be talking?' Ben asked hopefully.

'Making little talky noises…but not words.'

'I'll help him with his words,' Ben said solemnly. 'I'r
his big brother.'

Slowly they wended their way back indoors. Freddy l
their nanny take charge of the children and as she wer
upstairs to change for dinner she was thinking about wha
an eventful year it had been.

Just a month after she had discovered that she was ex
pecting Kareem, she and Jaspar had enjoyed a full churc
blessing of their marriage and her father-in-law had off
cially bestowed the title of Princess on her. She had bee
very relieved that she'd been still able to fit herself into
beautiful wedding dress for the blessing ceremony and th
service, which had been attended by so many people.

Six months ago, Sabirah had married a wealthy Lebanes
tycoon and had left the country. All of Jaspar's relative
had issued a collective sigh of relief at the knowledge tha
the power-hungry brunette would not be returning to th
royal household.

Ruth had come to stay with Freddy and Jaspar severa
times and she and Jaspar got on very well. Freddy ha
particularly appreciated the older woman's calm whil
she'd been carrying Kareem for Jaspar had been madder
ingly prone to panicking at her every minor twinge durin
her pregnancy. However, her husband had got over hi
aversion to hospitals fast once he'd realised that the onl
person he trusted to reassure him about his wife's healt
was her gynaecologist. But Kareem had been born at th
royal palace with a full complement of medical staff an
every piece of emergency equipment known to man stand
ing by. Jaspar had suffered a great deal more durin
Freddy's brief labour than she felt she herself had.

'That I should have put you through *that*...' he ha
groaned, wrung out in the aftermath and clinging to he
hand as though she had come through a near-death expe

rience. 'Never again, never ever again. I had no idea what it would entail.'

It had been very hard not to laugh and hurt his feelings, but it was pretty fabulous to be loved and needed and appreciated to that extent. But then she loved him every bit as much, she thought tenderly as she dressed for dinner, donning a turquoise designer gown with an off-the-shoulder neckline. She picked through her collection of jewellery. Some of it dated back hundreds of years and other more delicate pieces were gifts from Jaspar. Her father-in-law, who had recovered his health rapidly over the past year, was equally generous to her and she had become very fond of the older man. She liked the fact that Jaspar's family was close and had begun to think of his family as being her own.

Her aquamarine gaze shadowed on the awareness that the twin sisters she had learned existed a year earlier were still as lost to her as they had ever been. Time moved on, but with it Freddy's longing to be reunited with the only relatives she had left alive grew stronger. She would find herself dreaming about her sisters as she imagined them to be and then waking up feeling foolish, for how could she picture sisters she had never seen? As far as had been established, the twins appeared to have been adopted. However, the adoption agency used had been a private one that no longer existed and the stored records that had at first seemed to offer some hope had proved to be incomplete.

'I've got a surprise for you. Close your eyes,' Jaspar murmured huskily from the doorway.

Freddy stole an appreciative glance at him in the mirror. He was lounging back against the door and looking drop-dead gorgeous.

'You're cheating.'

'I haven't seen you all day but if you've got me more fudge, I'll kill you,' she muttered, lowering her lashes.

'Is it my fault you can't resist temptation, *ma belle*?'

Even his voice still sent little shivers through her in certain moods. Yes, it *was* his fault that she found him quite irresistible, not that she had any quarrel with that. Going to bed with an irresistible guy every night was not the stuff of complaint.

'Keep on smiling like that and we might never make it downstairs to dinner,' Jaspar warned.

Her smiled just got bigger and bigger and bigger.

'You shameless hussy, you,' Jaspar muttered raggedly as he spun her round to face him and claimed a hungrily sensual kiss, only to set him back from her again with a rueful groan. 'But this is important.'

Surfacing from that far too brief embrace, Freddy gazed up at him in bemused enquiry. 'What is?'

'One of your sisters has been identified...now, don't get too excited,' Jaspar warned her levelly, dark golden eyes serious. 'This is old information and we might have a name but we don't have an address or anything else.'

Totally ignoring his initial warning, Freddy gasped joyously. 'What's her name?'

'Melissa. She's the elder twin and she goes by your mother's maiden name, Carlton. We know where she was living at the age of five but, so far, nothing further has been established.'

'But if we've got her name...that's a great start!'

'So it is,' Jaspar agreed, his brilliant gaze nailed to her excited face and his arms tightened possessively and protectively round her, for she had such high hopes.

'I love you so much,' Freddy told him with her heart in her eyes. 'I can feel in my bones that we're going to find her!'

Jaspar anchored long fingers into her tumbling blonde

mane. 'I love you too. I also tucked Ben into bed on the way in here and Kareem is fast asleep.'

'You're so organised.' Freddy turned pink.

'And you are so willing to *be* organised, *ma belle*,' Jaspar teased with a husky laugh of appreciation. 'Did I ever tell you how wonderful you are?'

'You can't tell me often enough.' Freddy quivered against his tall, well-built frame as he extracted a lingering kiss that sent her temperature rocketing, and dinner was very, very late that evening.

Princes...Princesses...
London Castles...New York Mansions...
To live the life of a royal!

**In 2002, Harlequin Books lets you escape to a
world of royalty with these royally themed titles:**

**Celebrate a year of royalty with
Harlequin Books!**

Available at your favorite retail outlet.

HARLEQUIN®
Makes any time special ®

Visit us at www.eHarlequin.com

HSROY02

The world's bestselling romance series.

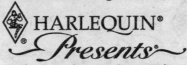

HARLEQUIN®
Presents

Seduction and Passion Guaranteed!

A new trilogy by **Carole Mortimer**

BACHELOR
COUSINS

Three cousins of Scottish descent...they're male, millionaires and marriageable!

Meet Logan, Fergus and Brice, three tall, dark, handsome men about town. They've made their millions in London, but their hearts belong to the heather-clad hills of their grandfather McDonald's Scottish estate.

Logan, Fergus and Brice are about to give up their keenly fought-for bachelor status for three wonderful women— laugh, cry and read all about their trials and tribulations in their pursuit of love.

To Marry McKenzie
On-sale July, #2261

Look out for:
To Marry McCloud
On-sale August, #2267

To Marry McAllister
On-sale September, #2273

Pick up a Harlequin Presents novel and you will enter a world of spine-tingling passion and provocative, tantalizing romance!

HARLEQUIN®
Makes any time special ®

Available wherever Harlequin books are sold.

HARLEQUIN *Presents*

The world's bestselling romance series… The series that brings you your favorite authors, month after month:

Helen Bianchin
Emma Darcy
Lynne Graham
Penny Jordan
Miranda Lee
Sandra Marton
Anne Mather
Carole Mortimer
Susan Napier
Michelle Reid

and many more uniquely talented authors!

Wealthy, powerful, gorgeous men…Women who have feelings just like your own… The stories you love, set in glamorous, international locations

HARLEQUIN PRESENTS®
Seduction and passion guaranteed!

Available wherever Harlequin books are sold.